Praise for Tracy Holczer

★ "Affectingly tracing Lucy's struggles with her altered family, Holczer also credibly portrays the conflicting views on the war, from protestors to former vets. Well-grounded in its era and peopled by fully realized characters, the book is **a resonant historical novel** and a **thoughtful exploration of how war and injury affect family, friendships, and individual growth.**"
—*Publishers Weekly*, **starred review**
of *Everything Else in the Universe*

"Lucy's adjustments are thoughtfully examined, and her evolving efforts to stabilize her family in general, and her father in particular, are **well crafted** . . . **Holczer does a fine job of piercing the weight with bits of family levity,** and with the ethereal beauty of the dragonflies—Milo's obsession—that flit in and out of the story."
—*Booklist* on
Everything Else in the Universe

★ "**A lovely and captivating debut** . . . nuanced characters engage from beginning to end."
—*Publishers Weekly*,
starred review of *The Secret Hum of a Daisy*

"**Lyrically written,** the novel portrays the war's corrosive, divisive impacts with compassion . . . **A touching, memorable read** that explores the costs, large and small, of an unpopular war."
—*Kirkus Reviews* on *Everything Else in the Universe*

★ "Holczer expertly crafts the characters and dialogue to create a story readers will identify with, and thoroughly enjoy."
—*School Library Journal*, **starred review** of *The Secret Hum of a Daisy*

"The novel introduces **a nuanced view of the Vietnam War to readers** . . . This is **a quiet, tender work of historical fiction about grief, love, and learning to let go** . . . A worthy addition to any middle grade collection." —*School Library Journal* on *Everything Else in the Universe*

"In this debut novel, Holczer presents **a tender, transformative exploration of family, loss and reconciliation.**"
—*Kirkus Reviews* on *The Secret Hum of a Daisy*

"Holczer weaves healing symbols . . . and poetry into her lyrical text . . . in this **heartfelt debut about loss and love.**"
—*The Horn Book* on *The Secret Hum of a Daisy*

"Readers who appreciate the quiet confidence and maturity of Cynthia Rylant's, Patricia MacLachlan's, and Katherine Paterson's protagonists will find **a new author to enjoy.**"
—*Booklist* on *The Secret Hum of a Daisy*

ALSO BY TRACY HOLCZER

The Secret Hum of a Daisy

everything else
in the universe

everything else in the universe

in the

universe

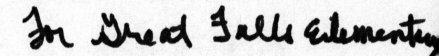

For Great Falls Elementary

TRACY HOLCZER

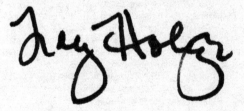

Trey Holczer

PUFFIN BOOKS

PUFFIN BOOKS
An imprint of Penguin Random House LLC, New York

First published in the United States of America by G. P. Putnam's Sons, 2018
Published by Puffin Books, an imprint of Penguin Random House LLC, 2019

THE LIBRARY OF CONGRESS HAS CATALOGED THE G. P. PUTNAM'S SONS EDITION AS FOLLOWS:

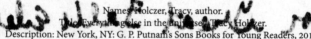

Names: Holczer, Tracy, author.
Title: Everything else in the universe / Tracy Holczer.
Description: New York, NY: G. P. Putnam's Sons Books for Young Readers, 2018.
Summary: In 1971, twelve-year-old Lucy Rossi's dad returns from Vietnam after losing part
of his arm, and her whole family must learn to adjust to a new dynamic, but Lucy's friend
Milo unknowingly helps her navigate through this difficult time of fear and uncertainty to
realize she is much tougher than she thought.
Identifiers: LCCN 2017057236 | ISBN 9780399163944 (hardback) |
ISBN 9780698173859 (ebook)
Subjects: | CYAC: Family life—Fiction. | Friendship—Fiction. | Amputees—Fiction.
| Italian Americans—Fiction. | Vietnam War, 1961–1975—United States—Fiction. |
BISAC: JUVENILE FICTION / Family / General (see also headings under Social Issues).
| JUVENILE FICTION / Social Issues / Friendship. | JUVENILE FICTION / Historical /
United States / 20th Century.
Classification: LCC PZ7.H6974 Ey 2018 | DDC [Fic]—dc23
LC record available at https://lccn.loc.gov/2017057236
Puffin Books ISBN 9780147508478

Printed in the United States of America

Design by Jaclyn Reyes
Text set in Adobe Devanagari

1 3 5 7 9 10 8 6 4 2

For my Italian family, who let me in

Mal comune, mezzo gaudio.

A shared trouble is half joy.

everything else
in the universe

stuck like a fish

a pale green balloon shaped like a fish was trapped in the branches of the willow tree down by the creek. A trout, maybe. From her bedroom window, Lucy watched it flutter there, caught by its string, wondering if it might break free and go for a swim. She took an inventory of her garden around the tree, California fuchsia and morning glory, plants she'd carefully chosen over the course of the year for their hardiness and survival skills, a practical reminder that she would survive, too.

If she were a superstitious person, like the rest of her irrational family, maybe she would have seen that fish as a sign of good luck, or a gift from the heavens meant to bring her hope. It was a fish, after all, and her family was especially irrational about fish stories, the way most people were irrational about four-leaf clovers or wishing on dandelion fluff.

But Lucia Mercedes Evangeline Rossi was, most definitely,

not a superstitious person. She never threw salt over her shoulder, like Great-Aunt Lilliana, causing a slip hazard, nor did she believe that bird feathers in the house brought the evil eye. She didn't believe it was good luck to hear a cat sneeze, nor bad luck to trim her toenails on a Thursday.

Lucy had recently had the misfortune of watching the aunts chant over the youngest of her three cousins, all named Joe, who had the flu. They lit candles and put a tomato on his belly button.

A to-ma-to on his bel-ly but-ton.

And then he threw up all over them anyway.

It was proof that Reason should govern all things. Just like Dad always said.

Maybe if Lucy had grown up in San Jose with the rest of the Rossis, she'd happily wear amulets made of rue to protect her from falling pianos or unlucky eyebrows and she'd believe things "deep down in her Rossi bones." But she and Mom had been saved from all that, having only moved to San Jose when Dad was sent to Vietnam. Living first in Boston, then Chicago while Dad went to medical school and finished his residencies made them "resilient, well-rounded women" who were "not given to hysterics."

Although Lucy was a practical person, an orderly person, a thinker of thoughts just like her father, she had done three things repeatedly while Dad was in Vietnam. She did not see this as a ritual or superstition as much as she believed it to be a recipe of sorts, meant to make her feel better. Like Papo Angelo's square noodle soup.

Lucy had written it all down in an essay for Mrs. Peacock in sixth grade last year, arguing the importance of what she called her behavioral comfort routine—perfect for anyone who might be in need of a plan—which Lucy valued just as much as her poster of Mohs' Mineral Table of Hardness for her rock collection, or her entire set of gold-embossed *Encyclopaedia Britannica*, a gift from her father on her sixth birthday.

When Linda McCollam—with her flaming mustard argyle socks and plaid miniskirt—read Lucy's essay on the Open House board and asked, "Why can't you just be normal?" Lucy stared at her, dumbfounded by both the question and how anyone with flaming mustard argyle socks and a plaid miniskirt might be the one to ask it.

In trying to understand why self-important Linda McCollam, who was the actual granddaughter of Millard McCollam of Millard McCollam Elementary fame, would say such a thing, Lucy turned to her essay on the board and tried to see it from a different perspective. It simply detailed how:

1) Each morning, Lucy put a dab of Aqua Velva on her wrist to keep her nasal passages from forgetting the smell of her father.

2) Each afternoon, Lucy went to her windowsill and counted the small stones Dad had sent in each of his letters. He'd asked her to look up what sorts of rocks he was finding on the other side of the world, categorize them against Mohs' Mineral Table of Hardness and report her findings. Discovery: both sides of the world had the same rocks.

And finally: 3) Each evening, right before bed, Lucy stared at her favorite picture, the one of her sitting on Dad's lap, five years old with a rather serious expression, pressing a stethoscope to his chest while looking up into his face. She stared intently at this picture so she would remember Dad's clean-shaven face, the loud-slow thump of his heart.

After Linda McCollam had flounced away, Mrs. Peacock had come up behind Lucy and reminded her of the unit they'd studied on homeostasis in biology a few months before. *Homeostasis* was from the Greek word for "same" or "steady." It was the process by which living things maintained a stable condition necessary for survival. Lucy understood the process to mean physical survival, like the body constantly working to remain steady at 98.6 degrees, no matter the weather or hotheaded encounters with Linda McCollam, and so she hadn't thought of it any other way. Until then.

"Homeostasis isn't just about your physical condition, but your feeling, and thinking as well. Sometimes we need to do things that make us feel better, even if they don't make sense to anyone else."

Lucy was comforted by this and so began referring to her behavioral comfort routine as her Homeostasis Extravaganza.

All perfectly normal. Even Mrs. Peacock said so.

Lucy watched the creek bubble silently, the balloon still stuck, and turned on the small stereo next to the window, where she pushed a Beethoven eight-track into its slot. The

Piano Sonata No. 14 in C minor was especially relaxing as she counted her windowsill stones for the last time, placing them one by one into the empty cigar box she'd snatched from Papo's house. She then placed the bottle of Aqua Velva beside the stones, along with her essay and stethoscope picture, and closed the sweet-smelling lid, she hoped, forever. She wouldn't have to partake in her Extravaganza anymore because the waiting was over. Even though Dad was coming home changed, in exactly two hours and seven minutes, he was finally coming home, and everything would go back to normal.

But as soon as she slid the box under her bed, she went all jangly on the inside, as though her bones had come loose from their tethers.

Even though there was absolutely, positively no reason for it, she couldn't talk herself out of the jangles until she'd taken every single stone out of the box and put them back on the windowsill, in order of hardness, sprayed Aqua Velva on her wrist, and set the stethoscope picture back on her nightstand table.

All where they belonged.

For the first time, she wondered if there was such a thing as too much homeostasis, and if perhaps Linda McCollam had been right after all.

back on the horse

*b*efore Dad left for Vietnam, he and Mom ran a tight ship, and Lucy was a good soldier. Even though they hadn't been a military family yet, Mom and Dad believed that a proper schedule and good hygiene were the answer to a happy and well-adjusted life. Dad had been working since Lucy had been born toward being a heart surgeon, which meant school, more school and then more school after that. Because he wasn't home in the mornings and evenings like a regular dad, every precious minute of family time was accounted for.

On the few mornings he was home, he'd read *Scientific American* or the *Wall Street Journal* out loud at the breakfast table. When he'd finished, he'd start almost every sentence with "Lucy, did you know . . . ?" or "Come here, Janey. Look what they've discovered about transplantation."

Lucy loved that he started his sentences with *Lucy, did you know . . . ?* as though she might already know about the stock market or business trends or new technologies in science. She loved listening to his deep voice saying things like *aortic valve stenosis* and *hard capital rationing,* and loved even more that he believed she was smart enough to talk to about it.

When he'd been home on those rare mornings, he'd brought Lucy into his smart doctor world just as though she belonged there. Because they were a team. And not just because Dad talked to her about *aortic valve stenosis,* but because she had her own part to play in his becoming a doctor. A silent part, but no less important.

Lucy's part was that she had valiantly, if a little sadly, sacrificed her time with him. All the time she could have spent with her father reading books, riding bikes in the park or just eating dinners together at home. Instead, she and Mom would get on the number 4 bus that would take them across town so they could deliver Dad his dinner at the hospital. Sometimes they'd get to eat together in the cafeteria with all the other residents, who would play games with Lucy and always had pockets full of peppermints because they were her favorite. Sometimes Dad would be so tired, he'd barely wake up from a nap to eat the Tupperware of pasta Bolognese, and so they'd just kiss his stubbled cheek and leave it there under his cot.

It wasn't as though Lucy was entirely deprived, however. Mom made sure she spent time with friends' dads, who threw her in the pool and watched Saturday morning cartoons and showed her how to roast the perfect marshmallow. It wasn't the same, but it wasn't terrible, either.

Lucy didn't mind these sacrifices; they were her contribution to their team. Together, they were helping Dad become a doctor. When graduation finally came and it was time for Dad to walk down the aisle to accept that little certificate with the MD after his name, he took Lucy by the hand and brought her with him.

Dad said she'd earned it, too.

———

Because Dad had also trained Lucy to be a thinker of positive thoughts, she forced several of his favorites through her mind as she went into her parents' bedroom:

Progress is never a straight line.

Nothing worth doing is ever easy.

We should always seek to be an instrument in this life.

And he didn't mean a tuba or a violin. He meant, *Be useful.*

"Can I help?" Lucy said to her mother.

"Everything is going to be fine," Mom said, even though that wasn't the question Lucy had asked.

Mom was dressing for the airport, walking from closet to dresser and back to closet, gathering electricity through her rubber-soled slippers, flinging nylons and shoes and all sorts of unmentionables all over the place.

If Lucy hadn't known any better, she'd have thought Mom was worried. But that was impossible. Mom didn't allow words like *worry*, *nervous* or *try* into their vocabulary. They were

Chin-Up Women. Stiff-Upper-Lip Women. Just like Grandma Miller and everyone else on Mom's side of the family.

Lucy went around and picked up, trying to stay out of reach as she didn't want to get zapped with slipper-conducted static electricity. Dad deserved to come home to a clean room and to a daughter who was static free.

"Everything is going to be fine," Mom said again, exactly like a worried person.

Which was not good. Because worried people were unpredictable, and it was important to be able to predict behavior in the wild so that if you're watching a chimp, say, like Jane Goodall does, you can tell when they might want to bite your face off. Mom was always saying how Lucy was far too concerned with watching things and should behave more like a twelve-year-old, talking on the phone, wearing lip gloss and listening to David Cassidy records. Mom especially liked to remind her that Gia, her teenage cousin, had gone to a record-breaking seventeen birthday parties when she'd been twelve, and didn't Lucy think that a fabulous goal to set for herself?

Of course, Lucy would say, and show Mom all her teeth.

Like a chimp.

Once every last strand of Mom's beach-sand hair was safely pulled into a French twist, and her clip-on pearl earrings snapped evenly to her earlobes, she sat beside Lucy at the foot of the bed and pressed her shoulders back, lifted her chin.

"Things will be different when Dad gets home."

Lucy nodded. She'd been putting together a reference

collection of books with the help of Ms. Lula, the Millard McCollam Elementary librarian. At the beginning of the school year, when Lucy started spending her lunch period in the library, Ms. Lula had fed Lucy books like she was feeding a fire in the middle of an Antarctic freeze. When Lucy finally managed to squeak out that her dad was in Vietnam, and preferred nonfiction so that she might prepare herself for all possible outcomes, Ms. Lula brought in all sorts of reference items from her Giant Reception of Knowledge, or so she called it. Every once in a while, she tried to slip in something like *The Lion, the Witch and the Wardrobe*, but Lucy figured she didn't have time to lose herself in a fictional world when she had so much to learn about the real one.

Lucy had books on the Vietnam War, psychology and every copy of *Life* magazine going back three years to 1968. Ms. Lula worked part-time in the school library and part-time for the city library, so she had access to everything. More than President Nixon, according to Ms. Lula.

"Remember. Bad things don't happen. Only learning opportunities," Mom said, getting Lucy's attention. But for the first time ever, Lucy wasn't sure Mom believed her own words.

"Get back on the horse or you'll forget how to ride," Lucy said. It was Dad's favorite saying. Never give up.

Mom smiled. Corrected Lucy's posture, tilted her chin.

"Your dad will need some space . . . and time to figure things out. What he thinks is best, and what I think is best, may not seem best to you for a while."

"Of course," Lucy said. "I set up the walkie-talkies in case Dad wants to be alone periodically. Plus, there's the schedule I created in order to help him settle back into our daily routines. I gathered some things I thought might help with his physical therapy. I've read what I could on amputation, even though there wasn't as much information as I would have liked."

Mom flinched at the word *amputation*, while Lucy pretended the word didn't bother her. Mom took a deep breath, and then her hand was on Lucy's cheek. Lucy closed her eyes and tried to absorb every bit of warmth from her mother's hand.

When she opened them again, Mom looked right into Lucy's eyes.

"We're a team, Lucy. Always remember that."

Lucy hugged her stiff mom fiercely. Because even though the Millers found affection slightly troubling, or so it seemed, that was the only way the Rossis ever did anything.

And today, maybe the Rossis had the right idea. At least about that.

life is a meatball

finally, Papo Angelo's shiny black Fleetwood pulled into the driveway beside their new-used Pontiac, his older sister, Great-Aunt Lilliana, in the passenger seat. Papo honked and then jumped out of the car with a wave, a breeze blowing the seventeen hairs of his shellacked comb-over onto the left side of his head like a wispy sort of apostrophe. He quickly smoothed it over.

Mom walked into the front room. "Ready?"

"You look beautiful."

Mom smiled—the perfect doctor's wife—all blond hair and pearl earrings. But with Lucy's snarly brown curls and Italian nose, she looked like she belonged in the deli with Papo Angelo. Which was why each morning, she carefully twisted all that hair into perfect braids to keep it tame.

As Mom locked the bright yellow door of their small house, Uncle G pulled down the adjoining driveway with

Aunt Rosie and Gia—whom Lucy was barely speaking to at the moment—in the back seat. Even though he had a work truck, Uncle G's car was also stenciled with his company name and motto:

MICHELANGELO'S CONSTRUCTION
WE TREAT YOUR HOUSE LIKE THE SISTINE CHAPEL!

A parade of six more cars drove up, horns honking, small Italian flags waving from radio antennae. The whole Rossi family was going to the airport to pick up Dad. Every loud, honking last one of them.

But not the Millers. It wasn't appropriate to bombard an airport in such a way, and so they were waiting to drive down for the family party scheduled next month. Lucy had overheard Papo Angelo call them a bunch of bumps on a log and wondered if he thought she was a bump, too.

Lucy gave Uncle G a small wave. He owned the little house where she and Mom had lived while Dad was gone. He'd painted their door yellow to cheer them up, regularly brought Italian sausage that he had made himself and filled their house with big puffs of the only laughter they ever heard at home, usually at his own jokes.

Uncle G was Dad's older brother, and although she knew Dad loved him fiercely, she also knew they fought about Uncle G ruining his own life. According to Dad, he would have been a brilliant engineer if he'd just gone to school, and then he could have had a real job in the world, building important things like rocket ships instead of wasting his life building houses. Lucy had often looked around for the "blue collars" in her family that Dad talked about. She didn't understand what their collars had to do with anything, but if Dad said it, it must have made some sort of sense.

Papo Angelo held open the back passenger door for Mom and then opened the other side for Lucy. Lucy kissed him on both cheeks, as was his way. Lucy then took a peek over the top of the middle seat and saw Papo Angelo had brought Nonnina's brass urn, which was also his way. The urn was seat-belted into its usual place in the middle. She'd been gone two years, and he took her ashes everywhere.

Once Papo got behind the wheel, he said, "She should see her son come home, don't you think?"

"Sure, Papo," Lucy said. Even though she was most like a Miller, there were times she felt the Rossi part of herself stir. And this was one of those times.

Mom stared out the window, ignoring the question altogether. She didn't think Nonnina's ashes were reasonable.

Great-Aunt Lilliana leaned sideways and planted a kiss on Lucy's temple as she peeked over the seat, probably leaving a bright red smudge from her lipstick. "You are ready for this," she announced. And since she was Fattucchiera, an Italian witch, it wasn't a suggestion, it was knowledge. Or so she always said when she made grand pronouncements.

"Life is a meatball, Lucy. Always remember that," Papo said. Great-Aunt Lilliana grunted her agreement. Because a good meatball was all about the right balance of ingredients, and so was life.

As the parade of cars peeled off one by one, Lucy looked back at the sign she and Mom had made together and hung last night: WELCOME HOME, CAPTAIN ROSSI!

When they all reached the bottom of the hill, honking and carrying on as though they were a wedding procession, Lucy closed her eyes and tried to imagine Dad's voice when he'd told her *I'll always come back to you.*

But she only heard her own.

———

There was a small group of people holding hand-painted signs outside the airport doors, THOU SHALT NOT KILL and GET OUT OF CAMBODIA among them. The girls wore flowing dresses with flowered headbands, and the boys wore stripes, so many stripes. There was long, straight hair all around. It was a Prell Shampoo convention.

Gia wouldn't get out of the car.

"I won't cross the line," Gia said, arms held tight across her chest.

As a plane roared overhead, and Lucy stood there unreasonably afraid one might drop straight out of the sky and kill her dead before she had a chance to see her dad again, Uncle G turned into a bear right before their eyes. All eyebrows and claws, he growled at Gia to Get. Out. Of. The. Car. Now.

So much for Gia's great protest against the war.

Which was why Lucy wasn't speaking to her. Not because Gia was protesting; Lucy could tolerate some of the protests about wanting to end the war. Even she wanted to yell from the tops of her lungs, "IT'S NOT FAIR," that her father—that so many boys—had been taken away from their families against their will in the draft. No. Lucy was mad because she had overheard a phone conversation just two weeks before that Gia and a bunch of her Students for a Democratic Society friends were going to Travis Air Force Base to protest. And the only reason anyone ever went there was to throw things at the returning soldiers.

It was the reason Dad had flown in on a commercial airplane and not into Travis. There had been pictures on the news and in the papers showing angry protestors hurling rotten food and insults outside military bases across the country, and Dad didn't want the family to endure any of that.

Dad didn't know Gia was one of them, of course. No one knew. Uncle G and Aunt Rosie never would have stood for it. And for all Lucy's anger at her cousin, that Gia might as well throw things at Dad, Lucy hadn't talked to her about it, afraid she herself might become hysterical. Instead, she pressed it all down, cooking and crushing those feelings, like the metamorphic process of stones deep inside the earth.

Gia made a point of hugging each of the protestors as they sang "Blowin' in the Wind," and she came back to the family as though they were dragging her to her very own death. She'd been given a white daisy and put it in her long, blow-dried hair.

"I'm against the war, Lucy. Not Uncle Anthony," Gia said for the hundredth time, as if it were that simple.

"You have a funny way of showing it," Lucy managed.

Gia flipped her hair over her shoulder in response.

Finally, the whole Rossi family, all twenty-four of them, twenty-five if you counted Nonnina's urn, with their balloons and banners, walked through the San Francisco International Airport, the Hairy Uncles handing out cigars as though a baby had just been born instead of a nephew coming home from Vietnam.

They did stuff like that, made up their own rules. Like instead of giving her an apple to bring for the teacher on the first day of her new school last year, Papo Angelo had given her a meatball.

Who wants an apple if they can have a meatball?

I do, Lucy had thought. But then, because she was taught to be polite, she smiled and delivered that meatball to Mrs. Peacock, much to the delight of the teacher and consternation of the giggling, monkey-faced students, because what did they know about Italian culture?

Many cigars later, the Rossis eventually found Rotunda A and the Pan Am gate arriving from Dallas, Texas. Beyond the window, the blue-and-white plane rolled to a stop, and two men in tan jumpsuits wheeled the metal stairway to the door.

Outside, the asphalt shimmered in the mid-June heat, and Lucy was happy to discover a similar shimmering inside herself. In just a few minutes, it was all going to be over. A whole year of numbness and Aqua Velva and counting stupid stones and staring at pictures of Dad so he would stay imprinted on her brain would be over. Even if he didn't have an arm, he was still Dad. He could do anything, overcome anything. She was sure of it.

A little girl in a red dress was the first out the airplane door, and everyone blew their New Year's horns that Great-Uncle Lando had handed out in the parking lot. Joe, Joe and Joey, Lucy's youngest cousins, six months apart between the three of them, all threw confetti they'd snuck in their pockets, and Aunt Connie chased after them until Great-Uncle Joe Senior gave his scary-loud whistle, even louder than the New Year's horns, and stopped them all in their tracks, including Aunt Connie.

The world was staring, as usual.

Then they all went even crazier, cheering as more people walked down the airplane stairs. Mom stood right beside Lucy, stiff as taxidermy, and Papo Angelo took Lucy's hand. She bounced on her toes with anticipation.

As the last passengers left the plane, the family grew quiet as lab mice. No Dad. Lucy's heart turned into a hummingbird and flapped its wings against her ribs, flap, flap, flap.

"You sure you got the date right?" Great-Uncle Lando shouted because he was half deaf.

Great-Aunt Maria smacked his shoulder and said, "Of course they did!"

Then Dad was there, at the top of the airplane stairs. All bones and gristle—the aunts were already clucking about which pasta sauce would fatten him up the quickest.

Lucy took an inventory. Aside from his missing arm, the rest of him was mostly the same. Same rounded tip on the end of his nose and ears that stuck out just a little too far. There was a raised scar on his chin from a dog bite when he was four, and the sleepy Frank Sinatra eyes that Mom had fallen in love with, or so she'd said after a glass of wine when Dad was newly gone.

Lucy knew Mom had said to give Dad space and time, but she couldn't help herself. As soon as Dad crossed the asphalt and opened the big glass door, she broke free of Papo's hand, her mom calling after her, and ran all the way across the blue, blue carpet, through the line of surprised people fanning themselves with their tickets, and heaved herself into him, wrapped her arms all the way around his middle. The familiar smell of Aqua Velva was almost too much, and even though he felt different—hard where he should have been soft—when he whispered her name, *Lucia*, his one hand gentle against the back of her head, she allowed herself to cry.

"Come on, now," he said. "Let's show everyone how brave we are."

They walked together to where Mom stood.

"Anthony." She said it like an exhale.

He let go of Lucy and put a hand on Mom's face. Touched his forehead to hers. Closed his eyes. Lucy leaned into them both, and they squeezed in tight, an odd number of arms, and ragged breath, finally together again.

And then it was over. Dad took a step back, jaw set. He began to tremble, legs buckling like he was having an earthquake on the inside, a regular seven on the Richter scale. Lucy watched as he leaned toward his left to brace himself against the chair before sitting down, only to realize there was no longer an arm to support him. Papo Angelo and Uncle G caught him as he stumbled. Lucy's legs froze in place as the Rossis all talked at once.

"He needs air . . ."

"Give him a swig of this . . ."

"He just needs a little space. A few minutes," Uncle G said, sitting beside him.

Dad focused on the blue, blue carpet, which looked like a stormy ocean if you were to get right down to it. He was balled fist and clenched jaw and sharp cheekbones and slumped shoulders.

Scarecrow Dad.

"I'm fine," Dad said with gusto.

A hand in hers. Only this time it was Gia. Lucy wondered if holding Gia's hand counted as talking to her, but held on anyway.

She focused on what Mom had said earlier. How it was going to take time to adjust. That was all. They were Chin-Up Women. They were Stiff-Upper-Lip Women. They knew how to handle themselves. So Lucy corrected her posture and tilted her chin and took in all the flapping about and general melodrama of her family and realized he needed to see she was okay. That no matter what happened, she was a lighthouse in the stormy sea of their family. Just like her mother. Just like always.

Lucy's future played out in front of her the way some people's pasts do when they think they are going to die, and she accepted that future without regret, knew, deep in the place she'd guarded with her windowsill stones, what her purpose had become.

She would be Dad's other arm.

A perfect example of homeostasis.

4

starfish

*i*t had been a Sunday when Lucy found out about Dad's arm, or more specifically, that he'd be coming home without one. When they found out, everyone crammed into Papo Angelo's house, where all the aunts, uncles, cousins and family friends came to make exclamations and hug each other and contemplate how to best heal him using the old Italian ways. There was chanting, the stuffing of garlic into pockets, and Lucy had been festooned with charms to keep off the evil eye, or *malocchio*, that had so tragically ruined her family.

It was very dramatic.

And Lucy, in typical Lucy fashion, was very still as she watched her family carry on, like wrestlers, only with words. As they all slurped their soup around three folding tables that had been placed end to end and covered in a white tablecloth, the deep-down need to run came over Lucy, which wouldn't have made sense to anyone else, their own needs being to cling to each other like barnacles or plastic wrap. And needing something that didn't make any sense to the other people in her family was a sure way to get the attention of the aunts. And anytime the aunts turned their attention toward an ailment, real or imagined, it involved chanting, candles and the possible use of a tomato on your belly button.

So no way was Lucy standing up in the middle of the minestrone soup course to announce that she needed Uncle G to drive her to the tide pools the way her oldest cousin Sheila always announced her sudden and preposterous ideas. Like going to bartending school so she could learn how to make fancy drinks garnished with little umbrellas so Uncle Joe's pizza parlor could be more "chic."

But something happens to a person when they don't say a thing that needs saying. When a whole year's worth of body count numbers going up and up and up on the television screen, and the worry over whether or not your dad is one of them, suddenly come spilling out of the tight bag it was all tied up in.

It wasn't pretty.

So even though Lucy managed to wait past the minestrone soup course, the chilled chicken cutlet course and the pears and cheese, she exploded somewhere around the serving and eating of the Sicilian cannoli, not to be mistaken for the Northern cannoli, of course.

"Uncle G, I need you to drive me . . . somewhere!" Lucy said, much louder and more shriekified than the quiet, matter-of-fact way she meant to.

The quiet, matter-of-fact way she did everything.

And for the first time in possibly ever, the whole yammering table of Rossis fell silent. Then the three Joes, sitting side by side by side, giggled.

Before Lucy could see what might come next, she pushed her chair back, walked straight outside and slammed herself into the blasting summer heat of Uncle G's black Mercury coupe. The vinyl seat scorched the backs of her legs, so she pulled them up to her chest and held tight. Mom came out and stood in the doorway, her blond hair a little sticky around the temples. Because who eats minestrone soup on a hot summer day? Mom wasn't going to let her go, of course. Mom would have worn Lucy around her keychain if she could have.

But she just stood there looking worried as Uncle G walked past, placing a hand on her shoulder.

Lucy didn't know at first why she wanted to go to the tide pools specifically. And Uncle G didn't need to know, either, apparently, because as he slid into the driver's seat, all he said was, "Book 'em, Danno!" Which he said sometimes when he climbed into the Mercury because it was the same car that Detective Steve McGarrett drove on *Hawaii Five-0*. Uncle G liked to think he was a tough guy even though they all knew different.

So Lucy and Uncle G left the flat cement sidewalks of San Jose, drove over Highway 92, and stopped by the Half Moon Bay Bakery about an hour later. There they picked up a fresh loaf of milk bread and drove on to Martins Beach, a place Lucy and Uncle G had been many times together over the last year when he fished for smelt.

For a little while, they just sat in the car, tearing off chunks of the still-warm bread even though they'd just eaten lunch, because that's how it was with a good loaf of bread. They squinted at the sun reflecting off the ocean and watched the fishermen in their spring suits drag their nets full of small squiggling smelt up the beach.

"When a starfish loses a limb," Lucy said finally, "another will grow in its place."

"That is a fact," Uncle G said, scratching his close-cut beard.

"I want to see if we can find one with a grown-back limb."

Uncle G didn't chastise Lucy, the way Mom probably would have, about how rushing out in the middle of an important family gathering to see a maimed starfish in a tide pool in Half Moon Bay wasn't a Stiff Upper Lip thing to do. He just walked alongside, pants cuffed to his hairy knees.

They finally reached the far end of the beach where the flat lava-colored rocks of the tide pools shined in the sun. The froth of the waves settled into the nooks and crannies and then drained out, leaving behind all the best sea creatures. Hermit crabs and mussels, starfish and sand dollars. Shells of every shape and size.

"Look there," Uncle G said, and Lucy carefully picked her way over the slippery rock to where he was standing. Sure enough, there was an orange starfish clinging to the side of a swirling pool, one arm much smaller than the others.

"It's growing back," he said.

Of course it was. But what Lucy hadn't remembered about starfish was that their grown-back limbs were never the same. The new arm was usually deformed or stunted and looked nothing like the one that had been there before.

"Nature likes to fill the empty spaces," Uncle G said.

At first Lucy thought maybe she'd wanted to see the starfish because of Dad's arm. But as they sat in the warm sun and let the sand dry in clumps on their feet, she realized the starfish was more like their family and Dad was the missing arm, and maybe she was nervous for the way he might grow back.

"What happened . . . to his arm?" Lucy asked.

"There was an explosion in the operating room. He's lucky to be alive."

Lucky to be alive.

"He won't be a surgeon anymore," Lucy said.

"No."

Lucy was quiet for a few minutes watching the waves crash in and roll out. "If he's still going to be a doctor, he'll need to study again. Find a new discipline."

"I'm sure your dad will figure it out. He always does."

"We'll have to move again," Lucy said. "To whatever hospital will train him."

"You're getting ahead of yourself, Lucy. Let's just think about getting him home. Getting him well."

Lucy nodded, surprised by the pang of extra sadness. She didn't want to move. Much as her family drove her crazy, she'd grown used to them over the last year. Uncle G especially. But she would do what was expected of her, as she always had.

"Are you ready?" Uncle G said.

Lucy wasn't sure if he meant ready for Dad or ready to go home.

"Ready," she said, answering both.

With that, they stood, shook the sand from their clothes and walked back to the car. Lucy took Uncle G's hand, even though she was much too old.

Because nature liked to fill the empty spaces. And so did Lucy.

———

When Papo Angelo pulled up to their house from the airport, there was a boy sitting astride a red bicycle behind a tall, thick gardenia bush, one house over. He seemed to be watching them.

Everyone had decided Dad needed a couple of days of fortification before the family swarmed in again like they had at the airport. Great-Aunt Lilliana rode home with the other Belly Button Aunts to give Mom, Dad and Lucy some private time. As soon as Papo stopped in the driveway, Mom sprung out like she was an honest-to-goodness Jack-in-the-box clown. She opened Dad's door in the front, and Lucy was flooded with about a million memories of Dad doing the same for Mom. It was weird to see it the other way around.

"So this is the new car," Dad said, taking in the metallic green of the Pontiac.

"Well, new to us, anyway," Mom said. It had an automatic transmission so Dad could drive.

"I'll get your bag!" Lucy said.

Lucy looked again toward the boy as she rushed to the trunk. He had moved more deeply behind the bush, but was clearly watching them. She could see a glint of gold, glasses maybe, through the thick branches, and a fluff of corn-colored hair sticking out the sides of a blue cap. She wondered if it was Billy Shoemaker from around the corner or some other equally annoying person from sixth grade looking for a way to embarrass her, to call her Bossy Rossi as they had all year.

Even after all this time, she still missed her friends in Chicago. When the kids you knew at eight were the same kids you knew at eleven, no one seemed to notice each other's peculiarities anymore. Like Tabitha's habit of eating her sandwich from left to right, left to right like a typewriter, taking bites so small, she made everyone late to the playground. Or Rubin, who never wore anything but a red shirt. He'd probably told them all why at some point, but Lucy didn't remember. Trina liked to wear her soccer shin guards, not because she wanted everyone to know she played soccer, but because she had a habit of falling down unexpectedly and was happy for the extra padding. Then there was Lucy herself, who invented Strange Fact Fridays, where everyone had to share something weird they'd learned, such as the fact that a six-hundred-pound octopus could squeeze through a quarter-sized hole.

Lucy didn't know if it was the difference between fifth and sixth grade, Chicago and San Jose, or Illinois and California, but she just never found the proper footing with any of the kids in her class this year. First off, there was the hair. Lucy didn't know how it was possible, but it seemed every single girl, and boy for that matter, had beautiful, flowing, straight hair. Plus they all seemed to have something "extra" about them—extra teeth in their wide smiles, extra giggles or extra-long legs—take your pick. And since the Beach Boys went and made a song about California girls, Lucy didn't think she was imagining things. Stick skinny with electrified hair, she was the runt of the litter everywhere she went. Top that off with meatballs on the first day of school, and there just wasn't any coming back from that.

Plus there was perfect, straight-haired Linda McCollam, who was famous because she had the same last name as the elementary school. When Lucy had asked who Millard Mc-Collam even was, as his name was nowhere to be found in her *Encyclopaedia Britannica*, Linda had informed her that he had been a school board member for eighteen years and a famous agronomist, which was, Linda went on to inform her, a scientist who utilized plants for various functions, including sustenance, fuel and fabrics. Lucy found this fascinating, of course, but also found Linda to be slightly unwelcoming and a little full of herself.

Lucy worried that a person could forget how to have friends, the way you can forget a face after too much time away. Now that they'd have to move again, maybe she was simply doomed to friendlessness for the rest of her live-long days.

Mom walked with Dad up the front path, holding his right hand. They stopped and admired the sign.

WELCOME HOME, CAPTAIN ROSSI!

Lucy hefted Dad's bag out of the trunk with Papo's help.

"You keep an eye on your pop, Lucy. Tell me if you need anything," Papo said. "And tell me if the relatives are calling too much, bothering you guys. I'll give 'em one of these and one of these." He motioned a karate chop and a poke in the eye with both fingers.

Papo looked up the path as Mom unlocked the door. He used the palm of his hand to rub at his eyes before the tears fell, and this made Lucy's throat tighten.

"I will, Papo. It's going to be okay. He'll go back to school. Learn how to be another kind of doctor. You'll see."

But it was slippery, her sense of sureness. Like a fish in her hands.

"Of course," Papo Angelo said, and put his hand against her cheek.

Lucy stood alone in the driveway and waved as Papo drove off. When she looked again toward the gardenia bush, the boy was gone.

introducing gardenia boy

*f*or the last year they lived in Chicago, Lucy and Dad had a game they played with the stars. They didn't believe it was fair that the Greeks had all the fun, so they named the constellations after the Rossi family. Each night Dad was home before bedtime, which wasn't often, and weather permitting, they would climb up to the roof and lie flat on their backs, and he'd quiz her on the real constellations before they would have their fun.

Their last rooftop night had been a Sunday. Dad had just gotten a job at Stanford Hospital in California, and they were packed and ready to go. Lucy would miss her friends, and her apartment building full of friendly neighbors, but Dad finishing school and landing his first job was what they'd been working toward for all the years she'd been alive, and she was ready.

"Look," Lucy had said, after she'd correctly named Orion's Belt. "It's the Joes."

Dad pointed to the Big Dipper, or Uncle Lando's Pink Champagne Ladle. Because if he could ladle pink champagne out of a bucket, he would.

Cassiopeia was a collection of Great-Aunt Lilliana's premonitions.

And Dad was the moon. Not the sun. But the moon. Pulling the tides and keeping the earth on its axis.

Dad turned unusually quiet for a little while, and Lucy let him be. Being a thinker herself, she hated when people interrupted the flow of her thoughts.

"I have to go to Vietnam, Lucy."

At first Lucy was certain she hadn't heard him correctly. "What?"

"I have to go to Vietnam."

"But . . . but you're a doctor." It was all she could think to say.

Dad sighed and put an arm around her shoulders. Squeezed. "The army has something called the Doctor Draft. They need people like me to go over there and stitch people up."

Lucy swore she could feel the water she was made of, all sixty-five percent of her body weight, drain down around her ankles so all that was left was bones and scared. "But you can get a deferment! Lots of people get a deferment!"

She didn't exactly know what a deferment was; she simply remembered it from a conversation in class this year where Mrs. Lacey was explaining the domino theory, how if they let Vietnam have communism, there was no stopping it from taking over the world, the way one domino will knock into the next and the next until everyone was doomed.

The class then had a conversation about whether there was an obligation to fight for freedom, or whether freedom itself, to be able to do what you wanted, was more important. It turned out Rudy's cousin Morty had gotten a deferment a couple years back so he could go to college. And then the class all talked about how maybe that was cheating and Lucy remembered not listening much after that because she was trying to come up with an interesting fact for Strange Fact Friday.

"If I got a deferment, someone else would go in my place. That's not who we are," Dad said.

Lucy believed she and her mom and all of their family were more important than some person Dad didn't even know, but wasn't sure how to say that without seeming like a cruel and heartless person. Maybe she was a cruel and heartless person. Maybe that's exactly who she was.

"I need you to do something for me while I'm gone," Dad said.

Which made Lucy sit up straight and concentrate. Dad often gave her tasks while he was at work, meant to keep her mind sharp and busy so the missing wouldn't be as bad.

"I'm sure I'll get lots of letters about the big things that happen in the family. Uncle Lando will write about his boils, Aunt Lilliana will tell me her premonitions and everything in between. Engagements, babies. I'll get my fill of front-page news."

Lucy nodded, knowing this was true. He'd probably get more letters than anyone in the history of the army. Ever.

"But I need you to keep track of the everyday moments for me, all the small things you notice, and write them down. I want to feel like I haven't missed anything, you understand? We'll get through this like we get through everything. We're a team."

Dad was giving her an important job, a job sliced into the perfect Lucy-sized shape because he knew her better than anyone else. Better, even, then she knew herself.

As they lay there on the rooftop deck, looking up at the sky, she knew she would never look at the stars the same way again. They would forever be connected to her dad's leaving.

"It's the small things, Lucy. Thinking about one small thing at a time will help the days pass, and calm your nerves. Leave no stone unturned."

"Will you come back?" She knew he couldn't answer that question. But it came out of her, pushed through all the other words, like a splinter.

Dad kissed her forehead and promised. "I'll always come back to you."

———

So Lucy's father sent her stones in his letters to remind her of her promise. And she wrote him about all the moments she'd been collecting, a little bit every day, so that her letters were thick as books. She wrote about the tomato-on-the-belly-button event, and Great-Uncle Lando taking three giant gulps of what he thought was iced tea but turned out to be dandelion wine. How he'd laughed and laughed that night at dinner until he fell asleep in the pears and cheese, and Papo and Uncle G had to move him into the guest room. How Great-Aunt Maria was so mad, she drew a mustache on his forehead with indelible ink, so then he had two.

And since her father was sending rocks in his letters from Vietnam, Lucy had also become fascinated by collecting and categorizing. After she'd received a new stone, she'd consult her poster of Mohs' scale. In bright colors, the poster measured the hardness of minerals from one to ten; one was talc, easily crushed, with ten being a diamond, the hardest natural substance on earth.

She liked thinking about how calcite could be scraped by a copper penny, but fluorite couldn't, thereby putting it in a different category of hardness. How everything was measurable with the proper tools. She also liked thinking about what her stones had survived. Volcanoes and tsunamis and earthquakes. And because Dad's leaving for the war had been its own raging storm that had worn parts of her away—like her willingness to make new friends, her small measure of spontaneity or her ability to sleep—surrounding herself with posters of the natural world, like the igneous granite of Half Dome in Yosemite Valley, helped her imagine she would survive, too.

Now that he was home—sleeping days and pacing nights because he still had them mixed up—standing before those posters each morning had become part of her Homeostasis Extravaganza. That and transferring all ten stones from her windowsill to her pockets in the morning and back to the windowsill at night. This way, she could count them whenever she was the slightest bit jangly, which happened more often than she would have liked, but at least she had a system. She envisioned her heart encased in a fortress of stones, protecting it from unproductive feelings of despair.

Onetwothreefourfive-sixseveneightnineten.

Lucy busied herself counting her stones and trying to be Dad's other arm. She went around the house keeping one hand in her shorts pocket so she could figure out those things Dad would need help with, and made a list. Uncapping the toothpaste tube. All can-opening duties. Shirt buttoning, which she did when the shirts came fresh out of the laundry, so Dad could just shrug into them. Banana peeling. The list went on and on.

What Dad wouldn't let her do, under any circumstances, was help him take care of his arm. She knew the incisions were still healing, because he'd just come out of the hospital before he'd flown home. Lucy knew he had to care for the incisions and wrap the arm in gauze each day. But he'd lock himself in the bathroom, tending to his stump as though it were something to be ashamed of.

And the horrible truth was, Lucy was relieved he closed the door. She'd hugged her dad when he'd gotten off the plane, but she hadn't been able to hug him since, unnerved as she was by the stump as it had brushed her shoulder. She made up for her secret and disloyal feeling of unease by doing everything she could to help in other ways.

At first Dad was somewhat accommodating of Lucy's efforts. Then, about a week after Dad had come home, when Mom was at the grocery store, Dad sat her down on the back patio for lunch with a couple of cans of soda. When Lucy reached for both cans, he shooed her hands away. He set the can between his knees and popped the tab off.

"See? I can do it," Dad said, and handed her the bright blue RC Cola, which tasted good in the warmth of the late June day. "I need to learn how to do these things for myself."

Lucy stared at a drop of soda that stained his pants as she sipped. "I just want to help."

"I know you do. But following me around cutting my meat and pouring my orange juice isn't the best way. You need to be outside, or at the library, or the pool, or chasing after the Joes, even. Do something productive with your summer. That will help me."

Lucy knew the tasks themselves weren't important. It was the being next to him that was important. She wanted to absorb the sadness and anger that poured off him in contrasting waves of snappy comments and silence. Soak it all up the way a sea monkey soaks up water. Then maybe he could go back to being himself. Telling funny resident stories and laughing so hard, his eyes turned to squinty half-moons. Twirling Lucy around the living room to Neil Diamond while they belted out the sad lyrics to "Shilo." Teasing Mom when she overcooked the pasta, even though he knew Mom would bring him the overcooked pasta as leftovers the next day as sweet revenge.

Lucy also knew she wouldn't talk about her memories, her longing for him to be like his old self, because she didn't want to add to his burden. He had enough to think about without worrying about Lucy's feelings, too.

Just then, the doorbell rang, and Lucy was off her chair before Dad could even scoot back from the table. When she opened the door to the reddest-haired man she'd ever seen, who happened to be holding an arm, she gasped.

"You must be Lucy," he boomed.

He was forty-seven feet tall and about as wide. Lucy realized her mouth was hanging open in an un-Lucy-like fashion. She snapped it closed.

It was all very unexpected.

"Shouldn't that be in a case or something?" Lucy said, pointing to the arm just hanging out there for everyone to see.

"Got the case in my truck. But the point is to use the arm, not keep it in a case. Right?"

Lucy stood back and let him in. She'd known this day was coming since Dad had come home. Was glad for it. Studies had shown that the sooner amputees used their prosthetic, the higher their chances of success, not only with the limb itself, but in other areas of life, too. Lucy didn't quite understand the correlation between a fake arm and happiness, but studies were studies. She just hadn't expected the arm to come to their door.

"Name's Brady Fitzpatrick. But you can call me Fitz. Where's the stump?"

"Um . . ." Lucy was temporarily rendered mute. She simply walked him to the sunshiny patio, where Dad was struggling with his tuna fish sandwich. Lucy wondered if stiff toasted bread might be easier to manage than the soft bread that kept bending from the weight of the tuna.

When Dad looked up, he seemed surprised. And it wasn't easy to surprise Dad.

"Are you ready to get started?"

"Um . . ." was all Dad said.

Lucy and Dad, two speechless peas in a pod.

"I didn't realize you'd be coming to the house," Dad finally said, annoyed.

"Ordinarily I don't. But when Giovanni says go, I go."

"I don't need his help," Dad growled. "I don't need any help, for God's sake. I'm a doctor. I know exactly what to do for myself."

A large chunk of tuna fish plopped out of his sandwich onto the plate, and Dad tossed the bread on top with frustration.

"It's time to water your garden," Dad said without looking at Lucy. He wiped his mouth with a paper napkin that left little napkin bits in the dark stubble of his chin and upper lip.

Lucy was entirely confused. Wasn't this guy from the army? What did Uncle G have to do with any of this? She would have to ask him for specifics.

Reluctantly, she tucked her sandwich into a napkin and walked through the backyard toward the creek. She turned around just before she reached the gate. "Are you sure—"

But the sliding door into the house shut firmly on her words. They had both gone inside.

Lucy reminded herself, *nothing worth doing is ever easy*.

———————

When Lucy first saw the boy digging in her garden, she didn't recognize him as the boy from the gardenia bush. He was just a boy digging in her garden, like an ill-mannered barbarian. Lucy stopped halfway to the creek, unsure what to do next. Scream? Run? Throw something?

Stand there like a frozen ham?

The boy turned and startled. "You can't sneak up on a person like that!"

That did it. Lucia Mercedes Evangeline Rossi unfroze herself and stomped down the rest of the way to face the boy where she noticed dirt clods and dug-up plants on the shaded slope beside them. She felt a cork pop inside of her somewhere that had been holding everything in.

"What do you think you're doing?" Her voice carried. Possibly to the moon.

"Well, this here is what you call digging," he said rather calmly. His words had a slight twang. Southern maybe.

"This is my garden! You're trespassing!"

"Were you especially attached to the weeds?" he said.

She took a deep breath. "WHO ARE YOU TO DECIDE THE FATE OF A WEED?"

"That sounds like a philosophical question."

Lucy ignored him and took stock. He hadn't actually torn up any of her plants, but he had dug some holes nearer to the creek.

"You can't just go digging around in other people's gardens! What's the matter with you?"

"Well, first of all, I didn't realize what you had there was a garden."

Lucy didn't have the greenest of thumbs, it was true. And maybe there were more rocks in her garden than most. And perhaps she let the weeds grow, too, because they had just as much right to be there as the other plants.

"And second, I didn't realize the creek was part of your yard. I thought it was part of Alum Rock Park."

Technically, this was also true. Penitencia Creek was part of the seven-hundred-and-twenty-acre wilderness of hills and valleys that spread out behind their yards. But Lucy didn't see how that made any difference.

"I'm sure the park rangers wouldn't be all that happy with you digging around in their park, either." Lucy lifted her chin. Crossed her arms.

"But if this is your garden, isn't that what you've been doing?"

Lucy was temporarily rendered mute for the second time in fifteen minutes and almost boiled over from the frustration of it. She understood failure, in all different sorts of ways, but never with words.

"And third, your uncle said it was okay."

They eyeballed each other. Then, whatever air had puffed the boy up suddenly went blowing out. He stooped over and sighed. "Look, I'm just making room for some wildflowers. I wanted to give the dragonflies a better habitat. This was the first place I came to that had a lull in the rushing water."

He took a bushy plant sitting beside him and stuffed it inside the hole, which wasn't deep enough yet. "See? I'm transplanting black-eyed Susans, swamp milkweed and some lilies. Dragonflies like that. I read it in the *World Book*."

Of course he read the *World Book*. He wasn't the more sophisticated *Encyclopaedia Britannica* sort of boy. However, since planting a dragonfly garden was just about the most unexpected activity Lucy could have imagined him to be doing, she couldn't help but let go of her own puffed-up air. She knew good and well she wasn't mad at this random boy anyway. He just happened to be there.

"Dragonflies?" Lucy said.

He nodded and went back to digging the hole. "My name's Milo, by the way. Cornwallace. It's English."

"Lucy," she said. She had no intention of giving him all her names.

The boy was tall with suntanned arms and legs. He wore cutoff shorts, a billowy red T-shirt, black Converse, and a pair of large gold-rimmed eyeglasses that were too big for his face. Lucy suddenly realized he was the boy she'd seen in the gardenia bush when Dad came home.

"Hey! You were the one who was spying on us the other day!"

"I wasn't spying."

And just as she was trying to figure out what to say next, Milo's rusted shovel clunked against something metal down in the hole. They both peered in, and Lucy saw U.S. initials stamped on a rounded piece of dirt-smudged metal.

"I think that's a flight helmet," Milo said.

"What's a helmet doing buried in the woods?" Lucy said.

Milo carefully dug the helmet out of the ground, and as he turned it in his hands, brushing off the dirt, he uncovered a round symbol—a ram and a lightning bolt—painted on the back above the words "U.S. ARMY."

"It's an insignia," Milo said. He handed it to Lucy. "Some men wear an insignia from their unit or battalion. I've only seen patches, though."

"Did you learn that in the *World Book*, too?" Lucy said.

"Nope. I come from a military family. I know things."

He waggled his eyebrows at her.

The afternoon was turning slightly *Alice in Wonderland*. If a person-sized rabbit came running through the woods at that moment, would Lucy feel surprised? Or any feeling at all other than annoyance at the interruption of what was supposed to be a few minutes of peaceful gardening? What would happen next?

"Here, take a look," Milo said.

Lucy inspected the helmet. As she turned it in her hands, she felt a bulge in the lining, right where the forehead would be. "I think there's something inside."

When she peeled the lining back, three black-and-white

photos fell out. Even more unexpectedly, a Purple Heart plunked into the dirt. Lucy picked up the pictures. Milo picked up the Purple Heart.

The top photo was of a man in uniform with a little girl on his knee, about five years old. The second was the same man with the same girl and a boy who didn't look much older. The third was of a woman with windswept hair sitting on a sandy beach.

"We need to put it all back," Lucy said. It was a violation to have dug it up, even if the idea of reburying those pictures made her feel queasy. Why would someone have buried pictures of their family? The Purple Heart she could understand, sort of. It represented an injury. Or death.

"Why?" Milo said.

Lucy didn't know how to explain. "Because I say so. And it's my garden."

Milo clenched his jaw, but did what she asked. He placed everything back in the lining of the helmet as best he could, and then covered the whole shebang with dirt, shoveling with gusto. When the helmet was buried once again, they both just stood there, staring at the newly turned earth. The birds called to each other. The creek burbled. Finally, Milo reached for a large wishing stone and placed it on top, like a tombstone.

"Lucy! Come help unpack the groceries!" Mom called from their patio up the slope, shattering the moment of quiet.

"I've got to get back to Grams'," Milo said. As he collected his things, he went on, "Sorry about all this. I didn't mean any harm."

Satisfied with his apology, Lucy nodded and walked back toward her house. Near the top of the slope, she called to Milo, "Why were you hiding in that bush, anyway?"

Milo had already tossed the shovel over his shoulder, and just before he disappeared into the trees, he said, "I just wanted to see someone come home."

losing the moon

*L*ucy wasn't sure what Milo Cornwallace might have meant by wanting to "see someone come home." She wondered if he meant it in a general way, the way you might want to see anyone come home from being gone so long from their family. Maybe he was just as overwhelmed by the television news as she was. It was on everywhere—in people's homes or behind the cash register at the 7-Eleven—showing the bloody mess of things over there. Even worse was the daily body count for American soldiers, South Vietnamese and Vietcong the news programs kept on the bottom of the television screen, ticking up every day.

Tick, tick, tick.

Or did Milo mean it in a more personal way? Did he know someone in Vietnam?

When Lucy had first found out her dad was going, the war had been a faraway event happening on televisions she mostly didn't want to watch, and in conversations between adults she mostly didn't want to listen to. None of her friends had older brothers or uncles, none of her own cousins were of the drafting age, and so, like a fire in another building, it was a horrible and sad thing that never really touched her life.

But now it had happened to her family. Lucy wondered if it had happened to Milo's, too. And because Lucy's mind was the way it was—always on high alert—she couldn't let it go. Not Milo, and not the pictures she now knew were buried deep in her garden, which left her feeling slightly queasy. The unknown, to Lucy, was like a fanged creature that hid in her closet or under the bed with all the other monsters.

Which was spectacularly annoying. Because Lucy needed to focus on Dad while he considered their options for the future. And while it was true that Dad hadn't asked her opinion, necessarily, hadn't even talked to her about what he might do next, Lucy knew it was important to be available, to be right there should he need her.

She had accompanied Dad to the library on a couple of research trips and introduced him to Ms. Lula, who worked at the Berryessa branch of the San Jose Public Library during the summer months. At Lucy's request, Ms. Lula had collected stacks of reference materials for Dad to ponder while giving Lucy the newest *National Geographic* magazine, and a scattering of books on subjects she thought Lucy might be interested in. Rocks and minerals, fictional accounts of survival stories, *The Hobbit*.

To add to her reference book pile, as though the prosthetist had known Lucy's secret heart, Brady Fitzpatrick had left a fifty-two page manual behind that covered the history of prosthetics as well as modern-day uses and instructions. *Appendage Prosthetics*, it was called. Over the last couple of days, she'd memorized it, one of the most important sentences being:

A brief period of time between surgery and fitting the prosthesis is imperative if a functional stump, and thus use of a prosthetic device, is to be obtained.

Lucy had already known this, of course, having researched as much as she could. But it went on:

The surgeon and others on his hospital staff will do everything they can to ensure the best results, but ideal results require the wholehearted cooperation of the patient.

And Dad wasn't cooperating. At least not about the arm. He'd tried. Lucy had spied on him through a crack in the bedroom door. But there were so many buckles and belts that it was hard for him to manage on his own, and so the one time she'd watched, he ended up throwing it across the room into the corner with a bang.

So even though Dad had told her he needed space to figure things out on his own, Lucy knew she needed to encourage Dad to follow Fitz's guidelines in this particular instance. She would help him with the buckles and straps if he needed it. This wasn't the same as following him around and putting toothpaste on his toothbrush. This was important. He would be impressed that she had read the entire manual and had an educated opinion on the subject. At least that she could count on.

Lucy found her opportunity for this discussion in the middle of the night.

She woke to the sound of the sliding glass door skipping along its lumpy track. She had no idea what time it was. The fingernail moon was framed perfectly in her window, so she figured sometime after one in the morning. After putting on her quilted robe, she tiptoed down the hallway into the empty living room—wondering where her father might have gone—thinking about carnivals, of all things. How she'd made the mistake of going on the Giant Swing three summers ago when a small carnival had set up just outside of Chicago. Dad had taken her as a special treat, so even though she found herself terrified of most every ride, she hadn't let on.

But the Giant Swing had been the worst. Lucy honest to goodness felt as though the extreme up and down of that swing was going to kill her. Humans weren't meant to experience such things. It was unnatural. And so she'd gripped her dad's hand and prepared for a myocardial infarction.

When it was over, Dad reassured her she was perfectly healthy and that her heart could, and in fact would, withstand a lifetime of Giant Swings. But Lucy swore she would never attend another carnival and, therefore, would never again experience carnival feelings for the rest of her livelong days.

Then her dad went to Vietnam and it was like spending a year at a carnival on the Giant Swing. She'd thought it would be over when he came home.

It wasn't.

Lucy looked outside. It was dim, the moon just a sliver of light in the sky, but she could see shadows. One in particular sitting underneath the large oak tree in the corner of the yard.

Dad. Still.

The crickets hushed when Lucy opened the screen door. But her dad didn't move.

Lucy's heart was pounding entirely too fast as she walked across the grass. The shadowy lump under the oak tree was, of course, her father. She leaned down and touched Dad's shoulder just to make sure he was okay.

He startled and sat up. "What are you doing?"

"I couldn't sleep."

After a moment in which Lucy feared he'd shoo her back inside, Dad patted the spot next to him on one of Uncle G's old beach blankets. She lay beside him and willed herself to look up at the partial constellations she could see through the leaves of the oak. Something she had refused to do since Dad had left. His leaving would forever be connected to the stars.

His arm was warm against hers. She was relieved his stump was on the other side, and felt sick about her relief.

"All the men on base would gather in the mess to hear me read your letters. Did I tell you that?"

"You didn't."

"Maybe I didn't want it to go to your head." Lucy could hear the smile in his voice.

"Did you get all thirty-seven of them?" she asked.

"Each and every one."

"I took a few turns delivering meatballs for Papo Angelo so I could contribute to the postage."

"How did young Joey feel about that, you taking over his job?"

"He didn't mind. He's a good kid. He even gave me three dollars from his birthday money to help out and wouldn't let me pay him back."

Dad chuckled, a sound Lucy wished she could capture in a bottle and set on her windowsill with her stones. After a little while, Dad said, "Did I ever tell you about the summer I turned thirteen?"

"Was that the summer you worked in Great-Uncle Lando's orchards?"

"That was the summer I decided to be an orchardist, just like the men in my family going back to the old country. Pears and apples."

Lucy hadn't known her dad wanted to grow trees like Great-Uncle Lando and Big Papo before him. She'd only been told how hard Dad had worked to save up for school, and from such an early age. Saving even the pennies he'd find in the street.

"Big Papo used to say that sometimes, when he couldn't sleep, he'd lie in the very middle of his fields, so much like Italy. He told me that when things get tough, you have to remind yourself of what you've already built."

Big Papo and Nona had come over from Calabria in

1917, their tiny village so poor, they'd lived in a one-room house with dirt floors. They had a cousin who had settled in Connecticut, but Big Papo dreamed of the land he'd heard about on the other side of the country, the Santa Clara Valley with its orchards and land so much like home. He would build a life there, and his children wouldn't be hungry.

"I remember the night he said that. It was warm, just like tonight, and he was sipping anisette out of a flask. He gave me a taste, and I thought I'd set my lungs on fire."

Lucy lay there quiet, thinking of the piece of her dad that had come from Big Papo. Like a star in a constellation. How she had a piece of Big Papo, too, through Dad, even though he'd died before she was born.

Dad went on. "Big Papo couldn't read, so he insisted his children be educated. By the time my generation came along, it wasn't enough to just be educated. We were expected to do more. What he said was, *Chi ha più giudizio, più ne n'adoperi.* Basically, *From those who are given more, more is expected.* More is expected of us, Lucy. And so we will keep moving forward. I will find a different job, and we will put this behind us."

Lucy was overcome with relief. This was the first real conversation they'd had since Dad came home eleven days ago. He sounded more like himself. It made her feel brave, like she could talk to him the way she always had.

"Why won't you wear your arm?"

Dad stiffened beside her.

"Have you read the research?" Lucy went on.

"Of course I have."

"Then you know it's harder to start using the arm if you form habits without it. And people who lose limbs and wear a prosthetic are more successful in their healing and their lives. I read that in the manual Fitz left behind," she said, certain that Dad would be impressed with her knowledge. The way he always had been.

Dad leaned toward her and pushed himself up with the help of his left leg. It was awkward, unnatural. "Lucy, this isn't your concern."

"Of course it is! You're my dad. We're a team."

"Not in this," Dad said, sharp as Papo Angelo's meat slicer. Then he softened. "We don't treat you like a child, Lucy. But that's what you are. This is a grown-up problem."

And there Lucy went, swinging up, up, up on the Giant Swing, her stomach in her throat, the solid ground of her life growing small beneath her. They had always been a team. In everything. It was the only thing they'd ever been. Now, suddenly, they weren't.

Lucy reached toward where her pocket should be, to count her stones, but it was the middle of the night, so her stones were back on the windowsill.

"You should get some sleep," Dad said. He scooted away from Lucy and leaned against the tree trunk. "I'll be in shortly."

Lucy slowly walked back toward the house and climbed beneath her clean lavender sheet. She looked out the window at the darkness beyond, reminding herself of what

Mrs. Peacock had told her about homeostasis. That a person under conflicting stresses and motivations has to find a way to maintain a stable condition. Dad was just trying to find his way.

I'll always come back to you.

Dad had promised. And Dad never went back on his promises.

the thick of things

*a*s the end of June turned to July, Lucy continually tried to categorize her thoughts as the Giant Swing catapulted her off into the wild blue yonder. She was a planner and a plotter, and yet her mind and heart were smack out of plans and plots.

For the very first time in her life, Lucia Mercedes Evangeline Rossi was at a loss.

Of course she was a child. She knew this quite literally. But that didn't mean she couldn't handle adult things. She'd been doing it for years. In point of fact, many people in their family relied on Lucy for her skills as a reasonable person. She was forever being called upon to sort out fights among the Joes, categorize pantry items in Papo Angelo's deli, and generally bring a logical and insightful addition to family conversations. She was the levelheaded one, the one who read all the books. The one who didn't fly into fits of despair over a change in plans or a too-big helping of mustard greens on her plate.

Mom and Dad had trained her to be a critical thinker, and she prided herself on this ability. Lucy just needed to remind Dad how tough she was. She envisioned herself made of iron and steel and all sorts of other tough stuff. She would be like the stones in her pocket that had survived for millennia.

———————

On the Friday morning before the Fourth of July, while Lucy stirred the milk in her cereal bowl, contemplating another day at the library with Dad, maybe, or an afternoon staring at her parents' closed bedroom door, Mom bustled around the kitchen at a frantic pace. She wore a polyester skirt that showed too much knee, in Lucy's opinion, and she was trying to do too many things at once. She clipped an earring onto her earlobe with one hand as she wiped down the kitchen counter with the other, forgetting to put on her rubber gloves in the process, which would have caused Grandma Miller to give a three-hour lecture about both the decency of hiding knees and how gloves were meant to keep a lady's hands beautiful. And what would become of the female species if we all had farmer hands?

Eventually, Mom stopped all the things she was doing and sat down across from Lucy.

"I have a job," she said without preamble. "I have to go in and fill out some paperwork today."

Lucy blinked and reached into her pockets for the stones. "Well, this is sudden."

"It is. Someone Papo Angelo knows. They need a manager for an apartment complex. The same job I had in Chicago."

"I didn't know you needed a job."

"Just for the summer while Dad figures things out. Anyway, you'll be going next door to G and Rosie's starting today."

"What?" Lucy dropped her spoon into her cereal bowl and splashed her clean red T-shirt. "Then who will be here for Dad? Who will look after him?"

Dad might not think he needed looking after, but Lucy knew he did. He was still being stubborn about his prosthetic arm. Stubborn about tending to his healing incision. Stubborn with his words and affections. Lucy needed to stay. To remind him what he was working toward. What they were all working toward. To be a team again.

Mom glanced down the hall toward their closed bedroom door. "Dad can look after himself. You don't need to help him," Mom said.

"You sound mad. Are you mad?"

"Oh, Lucy. Of course not."

Unable to look Mom in the eye, Lucy stared at her Press-On Nails. Mom kept a drawer of prepainted nails so that when one would pop off to parts unknown, she'd have another ready to go in its place. Lucy took pride in finding the fugitives, in the small fern on the kitchen table, or the fruit drawer in the refrigerator, and presenting them to Mom with a flourish.

"Look at me," Mom said. "I'm not mad. But I will be if you don't get yourself out of this house. You need to have a summer. Go swimming with your cousins. Learn how to make doilies with Aunt Rosie. Categorize your rocks."

Lucy was sure this was Grandma Miller's fault, putting thoughts in Mom's head about what, exactly, everyone should be doing with their summer. She'd overheard Mom on the phone when she didn't think Lucy was listening, saying things like:

We're fine for the moment.

Of course I'll let you know if I need you.

No, I don't want to send Lucy right now.

Grandma Miller wanted Lucy out of "the thick of things" and believed Lucy was being damaged beyond repair by witnessing her father's slow recovery. As though Lucy were the house of sticks from *The Three Little Pigs.* And while Lucy knew Mom was, in fact, the house of bricks from the same nursery story, she wasn't sure that was true when it came to Grandma Miller. Grandma Miller was the type of wolf who could blow anyone's house down, no matter what it was made of.

Lucy felt no better than a plant, or a box of shirts, something easily moved from one place to another. All her careful planning and study, everything she'd prepared for in order to help Dad, had been a waste of time. He didn't need her. Didn't even seem to want her around. Neither did Mom.

"Can I at least check on Dad throughout the day?"

"Lucy, you are going next door. You'll be home each night. Dad will be fine without you. Do you trust me?"

"I guess so."

But for the first time in her life, Lucy wasn't sure that was true.

———

Mom packed a "few things" for Lucy to keep next door so she wouldn't have to run back and forth and bother Dad. She looked like a nervous bird being chased by something bigger, and Lucy was so mad at being gotten rid of, like she was an infestation of cockroaches, that she didn't even try to help. She couldn't believe Mom had gotten a job. That Dad didn't think he needed help. That unless Fitz was there to help Dad, the arm stayed in the case in the closet, its absence like a harbinger of doom.

When Lucy and Mom stepped out their front door, Lucy could hear the usual commotion coming from Uncle G and Aunt Rosie's two-story ranch. The noise echoed off the hills of Alum Rock Park. Music, shouting. A door slammed. The sprinklers went on.

"This is not going to be fun," Lucy said.

She couldn't help but think of that awful rhyme, *step on a crack, break your mother's back*, as she stepped on every crack in the short sidewalk until they reached Uncle G's brick path.

"When I was your age, Grandma Miller sent me away each summer to Ladies' Charm School. Two whole months! You think your cousin is obnoxious, you should see a bunch of girls who all want the Perfect Poise crown at the end. You're going to be fine."

As Lucy studied the bricks, she tried hard not to let the tears fall. They were Chin-Up Women, Stiff-Upper-Lip Women, and she would remember that.

She would show Dad how brave she was.

Lucy watched her mom out of the corner of her eye. Perfect French twist, perfect pearls. The way she kept fidgeting with those pearls. Mom wore a halter dress, her pale shoulders already turning pink in the midmorning sun. Papo Angelo liked to say that Mom was a swan in a pond full of ducks, and they couldn't blame her for being a swan. But in her darkest corners, Lucy did sometimes.

The front door opened just as they reached the porch, Uncle G filling up the doorway wearing a brightly flowered apron and flailing a spatula.

"Just in time for pigs in a blanket!"

Mom handed Uncle G a heavy canvas bag. "Now, there's cream in there in case of a rash. And baby aspirin, as she tends to get mild headaches—"

"Moooommmm!" Lucy said, trying to take the bag. "I'm not an infant."

"No more than two per day. I've included her favorite eight-track of Beethoven, which she listens to sometimes in order to relax. She's got her zinc oxide for the sun, and her sun hat. Don't let her forget, or her nose will burn, then there's—"

Uncle G put his hand on Mom's shoulder, which miraculously pressed her Off button.

"We've got this," he said.

Mom turned to Lucy and squeezed her tight, then took her by the shoulders. "Be good. Okay? Listen to Uncle G and Aunt Rosie. I'll see you later."

"Okay."

Mom glided down the walkway and onto the sidewalk, catching the toe of her pointy shoe where the bricks met the concrete. A bird squawked in a tree just above.

Uncle G's brand-new SmokeGuard 700 went off somewhere inside the house.

"Darn that contraption!" Aunt Rosie yelled.

Lucy couldn't believe Mom was leaving her in the middle of all this pandemonium and disorder. She reminded herself again that *nothing worth doing is ever easy* as she stood in the doorway, one hand in each pocket, clutching as many stones as she could, her only defense against the world.

serendipity is not a hair product

*a*unt Rosie swatted at the smoke detector with a broom until it stopped howling and then pulled Lucy into a tight hug while Cannoli, their pillow-sized tortoiseshell cat, brushed herself against Lucy's ankle. Aunt Rosie smelled like flour and Rose Milk, and Lucy was grateful she'd grown tall enough that her face no longer pressed into Aunt Rosie's rather large bosom.

"We'll get you fixed right up!" Aunt Rosie declared, as though Lucy were a broken coffee mug. "Gia!"

For a long time, years and years, Gia and Lucy had been pen pals. Five years older than Lucy, Gia had sent school pictures that Lucy kept in a scrapbook with all Gia's letters and recipes, magazine cutouts and drawings. Gia had come to visit each summer, having been close to Dad, who used to babysit her when he was in high school, and Lucy would in turn visit Uncle G and Aunt Rosie. Gia was like an older sister, which was why her secret protest at Travis Air Force Base had felt like such a betrayal.

Because they had entwined over the years, the way the trunks of trees will if planted too close together, Gia knew everything about Lucy. She knew Lucy was terrified of the wigs propped on their Styrofoam heads in her mother's closet, but would cup a spider in her hand, and that while Lucy had never believed in Santa Claus, she had admitted to believing in the Cuckoo for Cocoa Puffs bird and Lucky Charms leprechaun when she was in the first grade. And Lucy knew everything about Gia, her obsession with palomino horses and how she was saving all her money for a white fringed vest so she could be a rodeo star, which then turned into an obsession with being a Pan Am stewardess. Gia had written those facts into her letters a couple of times a month for years. Then they trickled down to once per month, and then once every couple of months, and then stopped altogether when Lucy and Mom moved out from Chicago. At seventeen and in high school now, Gia sometimes talked to Lucy the way she talked to the other babies in the family, as though she were still a kid. Lucy's cousin was gone, and a Prell commercial model had taken her place.

"Hey, cuz," Gia said, and gave Lucy a pat on the head. She took the canvas bag from Uncle G. "C'mon."

"Come right back! We made pigs in a blanket!" Aunt Rosie called from the stove, and Gia sniffed with irritation.

Gia led Lucy toward the downstairs bedrooms. "We're

going to be pigs in a blanket if we keep eating like that," she whispered.

"Well, I, for one, love pigs in a blanket." Lucy sniffed right back.

Gia led her down the hallway, turned right—past her room—and kept going, straight into Uncle G's office at the end of the hall. There, a pullout sofa had been heaped with pillows across from Uncle G's cluttered desk. Cannoli leapt into the middle of the pillows, blending with all the fluff, and promptly rolled onto her back, as usual, expecting a tummy rub. Cannoli was the only cat Lucy had ever known who was so trusting, and she wondered, not for the first time, if she hadn't been given the proper amount of cat marbles.

"Mom thought you might like your own space."

Lucy took in her surroundings and figured it would be best that she stayed out of Gia's room anyway, because Gia had hung her protest signs on her wall. LOVE NOT WAR and THEY CAN'T KILL US ALL! Lucy didn't want to see them, afraid that in a moment of anger, she might just rip them to shreds. Not that she was prone to hysterical anger, but she did have fifty percent Rossi bones after all, even if she couldn't feel them mostly, and she couldn't be too careful.

"Mom cleaned out a drawer so you can keep some extra clothes," Gia said, twisting her hair around one finger. She'd taken to wearing Easter-egg-colored lipsticks, today powder blue.

"Girls!" Aunt Rosie shouted from the kitchen.

"Are you ready to tell me why you're so mad at me?" Gia said.

"No."

"Well, I made you this anyway," Gia said, and tied a braided piece of cobalt-blue yarn around her wrist. "Peace?"

Lucy scratched Cannoli on her tummy. There was a piece of cobalt yarn tied around her collar.

"Yes, even you, Cannoli," Gia said as she rubbed her tummy, too.

"I'll think about it," Lucy said. She knew she needed to talk to her cousin. Probably should have already, but she'd had enough to worry about without adding Gia to the list.

Gia flicked one of Lucy's braids. "Coming, Ma!"

———————

As Lucy helped Aunt Rosie and Uncle G clean the kitchen, Gia played James Taylor on her record player at an obnoxious volume. During the short ten minutes it took to clean, three of Gia's giddy-goose friends came through the door, one by one, without knocking, and made a beeline for Gia's room.

Why did Gia have to have so many friends, anyway?

And then Josh showed up.

"Hey, Lucy," he said, and pulled her right braid, like he did every time he saw her.

Lucy's face was warm, as though she were sitting in a beam of sunlight.

Because although she had tried repeatedly not to be in love with her cousin's boyfriend, it was hopeless. Joshua Giovanioli made Lucy's heart swell up into her throat so that she was about to choke all the time. It was a miracle she had survived the last six months at all. He was tall, at least six feet, skinny as a reed, so that Aunt Rosie was constantly chasing him with cacciatore chicken legs and such, and had dimples on his cheeks that gave Lucy the urge to poke her finger right into the middle of one.

"Do you want to go to the beach with Gia and her friends?" Aunt Rosie said.

Lucy couldn't imagine anything worse than sitting for an entire day in the baking sun with a bunch of giddy-goose girls, even if Josh would be there.

"That's okay, Aunt Rosie. I'll just work in my garden for a little while."

But Uncle G had other ideas. After they finished cleaning, Uncle G motioned for her to follow him into the garage. "You can help me pack up my tools for the day."

Uncle G loaded her arms with as much as she could carry out to the truck. "Why did you tell that Milo kid he could go digging around in my garden?" Lucy said as she stacked it all in the back of the truck.

"What garden?" Uncle G said with a wink.

"It's a garden!"

Uncle G laughed his deep belly laugh. "He asked if he could put in some plants to attract the dragonflies. He explained that the creek pools there, so it was the only place that would work. Dragonflies like the calm water."

"Why's he so obsessed with dragonflies?"

Uncle G took his tool belt off the work table and handed it to Lucy. "Why don't you ask him?"

"I don't know where he lives."

"That's Glenna Bartolo's grandson. He's visiting for the summer from North Carolina."

Glenna Bartolo was a nice lady who lived a couple of blocks over. Lucy had delivered meatballs from Papo Angelo's deli a few times when she'd been earning postage money.

"Maybe I have enough things to worry about."

"He could use a friend, Lucy." Uncle G slammed the tailgate shut. "And so could you."

Lucy rubbed the toe of her sandal into a rust stain on the cement driveway. She could feel her nose turning pink. "I don't have time for friends."

"What, you're so busy?"

She had been. But Mom and Dad had taken that away from her.

Uncle G scratched his short beard. "I know you want to help your dad. But sometimes, staying out of someone's hair is the best way to help."

"Are you saying I'm being a pain?"

"I'm saying you are in your dad's hair. He needs to figure out his own hair."

Lucy humphed.

"Milo told me you guys found some artifacts buried

next to the creek. Why don't you figure out who they might belong to?"

"How are we supposed to do that?"

"You're the one with the brains," Uncle G said. "Besides, what else are you going to do? You going to sit around all day and watch Aunt Rosie make doilies?"

It was true. They were everywhere: under fruit bowls, on every bed pillow, lying over the backs of chairs. Aunt Rosie said they made people happy.

"Listen, how about I drop you off at Mrs. Bartolo's? You can see if Milo is busy. And I may have a place for you to start your search for the owner of that helmet. What do you say?"

"Do I have a choice?"

Lucy glanced across the side yard toward her own house just as Fitz pulled up to the curb in a beat-up-looking Ford. He got out and waved as he walked up the front path for his twice-per-week visit. Lucy was jealous because Dad let Fitz help him with the prosthetic arm while Lucy wasn't even allowed in the room. She supposed it was Fitz's job after all, to make sure the prosthetic fit perfectly, to train Dad on how to use the arm and how to care for his stump. But the facts didn't make her feel any better.

"How do you know Fitz?" Lucy said. "And why did you send him? Doesn't the army take care of stuff like that?"

"I know lots of people. Fitz is a specialist, and no, the army doesn't take care of specialists like Fitz."

"How do we know he's qualified? Where did he go to school? What is his—"

"Listen, Lucy. I know you're worried. But this is one small thing you don't have to think about. He is well qualified and comes highly recommended from a couple of vets I know and have worked with. Good men who are helping their fellow vets however they can."

Lucy stared as her front door opened and Fitz disappeared inside.

Uncle G came up beside her, followed her gaze.

"Do you know what *serendipity* means?"

"Isn't that what Gia puts in her hair when she wants to make it straight?"

"No. It's the idea that you might find something truly wonderful, maybe even necessary, while looking for something else."

"Sounds like something Great-Aunt Lilliana would say."

Uncle G laughed his deep-down belly laugh and turned them both toward the truck. His hands were thick, and she felt the calluses on his palm rub the top of her arm. The opposite of Dad's hands, which were long-fingered and smooth. Perfect surgeon's hands.

"Are you telling me that by trying to figure out one mystery, I might discover ways to help Dad?" Lucy said.

Uncle G opened the door for Lucy, and she climbed in. He looked at her long and hard.

"I'm saying that you never know where the answers will come from. Sometimes you even discover you're asking the wrong questions."

Lucy wasn't in the mood for a philosophical discussion.

But she did recognize that she was at a dead end. Dad acted as though he didn't need her around, so it was up to her to find a way to convince him he was wrong. That she wasn't just a child who couldn't handle things. And maybe, just maybe, the answer was out there somewhere, and she would find it while doing something else.

Serendipity. She liked the sound of that, even if it did sound slightly superstitious.

mac and cheese

rs. Bartolo's house, down the hill from Uncle G's, had a pointy witch-cottage roof and a lazy garden with lingering vines along the fences and loose-leafed plants that intertwined and fell away from each other like green waterfalls. There wasn't a hedge in sight. Lucy had loved it from the moment she discovered it a few weeks back when she'd delivered meatballs for Papo Angelo. There were lavender monkey flowers and red-branched manzanitas and a flagstone path that went off in different directions. A tire swung from the thick branch of a live oak, and there was an explosion of bird feeders. At the corner of the house, under one of the windows, were two large wooden barrels filled with water, water lilies floating on top. Flying all around the barrels was a heaven of dragonflies.

Mrs. Bartolo gardened her wildflowers in a bed just outside the shade of the oak. She wore a floppy hat, overalls and bright orange flowered gloves. When she stood up, her smile was welcoming, if a little sad. Milo sat in a short beach chair next to her looking through the pages of a sketchbook, all skinny legs and arms.

Uncle G shouted out Lucy's open window. "Okay if Lucy spends some time with Milo today?"

"Of course!"

Lucy opened the door just as Milo stood up. He wore the same cutoff jean shorts, an oversized red T-shirt hanging over the waistband. He raised a hand, and she raised one back.

"Lucy." Uncle G scribbled an address on a piece of scrap paper. "If you follow the creek for a little while, about a half mile or so, you should see the house I'm talking about. There are a couple of tents in the backyard. Tell them I sent you, and tell them what you found."

"Why are there tents in the backyard?"

"It's a mystery. Don't you just love a good mystery?"

Lucy did not like mysteries. She liked the answer to a good mystery.

"Remember, serendipity," Uncle G said.

When she hopped out of the truck, she slipped her hands into her pockets and quickly counted her stones— *onetwothreefourfive-sixseveneightnineten*—and some of the pressure went away.

"I was so sorry to hear about your dad," Mrs. Bartolo said as Lucy walked up. She wasn't much taller than Lucy and wore her long black and white hair in a loose braid that hung over one shoulder. She was tan, her skin the color of a Bartlett pear.

"Me too."

Mrs. Bartolo took both Lucy's hands in hers. "You and Milo will be good for each other—"

"Grams!" Milo shouted, startling both Lucy and Mrs. Bartolo. "There's a blue jay in the oak tree."

"What? Where?" Mrs. Bartolo hurried for the porch and grabbed a broom. She zoomed back to the tree and looked up through the branches.

"Grams hates blue jays. They eat other birds, and she won't stand for cannibalism, she says."

"Damned right," Mrs. Bartolo said.

Milo's sketchbook was open on the seat of the plastic chair, a red dragonfly drawn midflight. It was extraordinary. But Lucy didn't get to look long because Milo closed the book and shoved it into a canvas rucksack, then shouldered it.

Uncle G gave a couple toots of the horn as he drove away. Lucy and Milo waved, and Mrs. Bartolo circled the oak tree, thrashing the broom around and mumbling about no-good rotten cannibal birds and how she'd show them a thing or two with the business end of her broom.

———

Lucy explained Uncle G's idea about finding the owner of the flight helmet.

"Which sounds impossible, I might add," Lucy added.

73

"Impossible just means you haven't found the answer yet. That's what my dad says."

Even Lucy couldn't argue with that. "I don't like the idea of digging it up, though. It feels like digging up a body or something."

"Come on."

Milo led her around to the back of the house, which was just as colorful and lush as the front. There was a fenced vegetable garden, lemon trees and a grassy yard half as big as a soccer field. He set his rucksack on the round patio table and took his sketchbook out. He flipped to the back and showed Lucy a perfect version of the helmet with the insignia and everything. "We don't need to dig it up if it makes you feel weird."

"Wow. You drew that from memory?"

Milo flushed red as he pushed the book back into his rucksack. "I like to draw."

"I don't have any talents," Lucy said, although she longed for one.

"There must be something," Milo said. "Everyone has a talent. Maybe you just haven't found yours yet."

"I did take a mime class once. It comes from the word *pantomimus*. It's what the ancient Greeks called the person doing the mime. But I had more fun researching than actually miming. The teacher said I was too stiff. Plus I couldn't move my eyebrows independently."

Lucy considered her inability to move her eyebrows independently to be a great failure of coordination, and worked on it sometimes before she went to sleep.

Lucy and Milo walked side by side through Mrs. Bartolo's grassy yard, kicking up swarms of tiny spit bugs as they went, to the back gate and creek beyond. All Lucy could think about was Dad, of course. She wondered how long Fitz would stay, and if Dad was cooperating or being stubborn. *Appendage Prosthetics* explained the role of a good prosthetist was to keep the prosthetic arm well fitted and comfortable at all times. They were there to make sure the skin didn't rub raw, as sometimes it took a while for feeling to come back to the healed area and an infection could set in. But since Dad wasn't even wearing the arm, did they just sit there and stare at each other?

Onetwothreefourfive-sixseveneightnineten.

Milo picked up a long, thin branch and swished it back and forth at foxtails. *Swish, swish.* "Did you know dragonflies can fly on shredded wings?"

"I didn't."

He went on, "There's this one called a wandering glider. It knows how to use its wings to work the currents in the air. They ride the wind for thousands of miles and pop up now and then on ships far out at sea. If I had to be something else, I'd for sure be a wandering glider. What about you?"

"I have actually thought about this before," Lucy was happy to say. "And if I had to choose something other than human, I'd like to be a naked mole rat queen, because...queen."

Milo blinked at her.

"The naked mole rat queen fights herself to the top, the same way queen bees do. They live in small naked mole rat towns, and they have rooms in their towns for absolutely everything, even bathrooms. They also live for thirty years, and their incisors move independently, like chopsticks." Lucy held her index fingers up to her mouth and moved them around to illustrate.

The edge of Milo's mouth twitched. He was clearly trying not to laugh. He must not have tried very hard, though, because he quickly bent over with the force of it.

"Well, I don't see how it's any different than wanting to be a dragonfly," she said. Lucy picked at the cobalt yarn around her wrist.

Then Milo laughed all over again. "Maybe you could be a naked mole rat queen . . . who mimes?"

Lucy cracked up. She couldn't help herself.

Once they'd gotten quiet again, Lucy asked, "Why are you so obsessed with dragonflies, anyway?"

"I'm not obsessed. I just like them. Some people like keeping track of the birds they've seen; I like keeping track of dragonflies. It's something me and my dad do together."

"What's the name of the red one in your book?"

"It's called a golden-winged skimmer. It's the last one I drew before I left North Carolina."

"Why?"

"I've been drawing birds for Grams. She likes to hang them all over the place. She says they bring the outside in. Even though she already has the outside in. She's got more plants in her house than a nursery. She thinks they're helping keep her alive with extra doses of oxygen."

"Do you usually spend the summer with your grandma?" Lucy asked. She was curious about Milo, like why he'd wanted to see her dad come home, and if maybe he knew someone in Vietnam. But before he could answer, they rounded a bend along the creek path and Lucy saw the two backyard tents Uncle G had told her about. One on the right and one on the left.

"That's it," she said.

"Why are there tents?"

"It's a mystery."

The backyard was on a slope. Uphill from the tents was a neat two-story white house with a bright red back door between picture windows. Men sat at wooden picnic tables on a cement patio smoking cigarettes, playing chess or cards. More men sat in chairs under the trees, reading newspapers and magazines. One slept in a hammock. Eight in all.

Shabby men. Scruffy men. Men in need of scissors, razors and soap.

Just as Lucy and Milo reached the low backyard gate, two more men came out of one of the tents, struggling with a large rolled carpet. One was tall, bald and stooped, the other short, sturdy and wearing an eye patch. The tall skinny one looked like Ichabod Crane from *The Legend of Sleepy Hollow*.

Where, exactly, had Uncle G sent her? To her doom?

Milo said, "Maybe it's a body. I watched that on *Ironside* once." Then he waggled his eyebrows independently from each other.

"Show-off," Lucy said. "Come on."

As they let themselves through the rickety gate, an

enormous German shepherd came running at them from out of nowhere, barking and barking and barking.

"Doreen!" Ichabod Crane shouted, and dropped his end of the carpet. The dog stopped in her tracks, and sat, tail thumping the dirt. The man ambled toward her on stilt legs.

"You must be Lucy and Milo," Ichabod Crane said. He held out his hand for both to shake. All bones. The other man came up beside him. "I'm Mac. This here is my friend Rodney, but we call him Cheese for obvious reasons."

Cheese was black, the same black as his eye patch. He was missing the fingers on his left hand, the whole left side of his body covered in ropey burn scars.

"Giovanni gave us a call and said you'd stumbled onto a mystery," Cheese said. "Why don't you come tell us about it? You can help set up for the lunch crowd."

"What is this place?" Lucy said.

"It's a meeting hall of sorts. For veterans. Sometimes people need a place to stay, so we have the tents," Mac said, gesturing as they walked past. "We like to furnish them with carpeting and foam cots. You caught us cleaning house."

Mac and Cheese must been the vets Uncle G had been talking about. "People *live* in the tents?" Lucy said.

"No, some just pass through for a hot meal and a good night's sleep. Most come for the meetings. Every night. Six o'clock sharp," Cheese said.

Doreen had taken an interest in Milo, so he kept leaning down to scratch her behind the ears. These must have been the vets Uncle G had been talking about earlier.

"We're serving hot dogs and hamburgers today. How are you two at squashing meat?" Mac said.

"I am a champion meat squasher," Milo said quite sincerely. "My dad considers barbecuing to be a serious and important skill."

Cheese flashed them a smile lopsided from the scars. He handed Lucy and Milo a pair of plastic gloves each for sanitary purposes, and they got to smashing and seasoning, the same way her family prepared meatballs, at which Lucy was an expert.

"How do you know Uncle G?" Lucy said.

"Hired his crew to do some work a while back. He's been bringing leftovers from your grandfather's deli ever since."

Cheese lit the briquettes under the barbecue grill. "Your uncle said you found a helmet and a Purple Heart?" Lucy tried not to look at his burns, tried not to think about what might have happened. Only half his mouth seemed to work right when he spoke.

"We found them buried near the creek behind Lucy's house," Milo said.

Mac and Cheese both nodded as though he'd just said something normal and expected, rather than strange and mysterious.

Milo removed his gloves and took the sketchbook out of his rucksack. He flipped to the drawing of the helmet and insignia. He'd done a fine job re-creating the ram and the lightning bolt, from what Lucy could remember.

"Well, I'll be. That's the symbol for the Dirty Thirty. First airmen committed to combat in Vietnam," Cheese said.

"But why would someone bury a helmet? And pictures?" Lucy demanded. These were not things to bury, she'd decided. They were things to save. Cherish, even. Evidence of a job well done, a sacrifice made.

"Sometimes the men who come through here leave things behind. As a way of letting go. There's all matter of objects buried out in those woods."

"Leave things behind? But there were pictures! Of a family!" Lucy said, feeling suddenly like she was at the carnival again. If not on the Giant Swing, at least waiting in line.

"Not everyone makes it back to their family," Milo said.

Lucy took off her own gloves and plopped down on the bench beside Milo. She'd seen enough of the news to know that was true. But the way Milo said it made her feel it was personal. That maybe someone hadn't come home to him. He didn't say anything else, and she didn't know him well enough to ask.

Mac nodded. "Some men . . . they don't go back to their families. Or their families won't have them."

"Why ever not?" Lucy said.

"Going away for a year from your family, from your life . . . time goes on without you. And while you're gone, you survive events, sometimes horrific events, that you don't want to talk about with loved ones," Cheese said. "It takes up space inside of you, all those horrible things. So, people come here to share their stories. Sometimes saying it out loud makes room for the good things again, like family and hope."

Lucy had been so consumed with the worry that Dad

might die or go missing in action that she hadn't considered the war might turn him into someone who would leave his family. That whatever he experienced might take up too much space inside of him so that there wasn't any room left for her and Mom. Lucy looked again at each of the men sitting around the tables and wondered if any of them had families they'd left. And if so, did it happen slowly, or all at once? Did their wives and daughters wake up one day to find them gone?

Suddenly, she was furious with Uncle G, and terrified of this new possibility. What in the world was Uncle G thinking by sending her here?

"How can you make someone stay with their family?" Lucy said.

Mac turned his palms toward the sky. "I wish I knew, Lucy. Wouldn't that be something?"

Doreen leaned against Milo, her head in his lap as they all sat in silence.

"I have a German shepherd, too," Milo said. "Her name's Lola."

Lucy reached out and scratched Doreen behind an ear. Doreen was smelly and had bad breath, but she was a comfort. Lucy had never had a pet. "I'm sorry. You must miss her an awful lot."

"You come visit Doreen whenever you want, son," Cheese said to Milo. He flopped the burgers on the grill, where they began to sizzle. "She's a good dog. Always knows the ones who need her most."

Lucy felt like a sack of broken crackers on the inside, all

loose and crumbly. And when she felt like a sack of broken crackers, her mind turned to the small things around her. Those things Dad had asked her to pay attention to while he'd been gone in order to calm her nerves. So she counted her stones and closed her eyes and breathed in the scent of grilling hamburgers, a smell that felt like summer. She opened her eyes and watched as a man stood up from the picnic table, stretched his arms over his head, and then helped another man steer his wheelchair over the lumpy roots of the oak tree. She listened to the trickle of Penitencia Creek in the distance, the hush of leaves in the trees all around them, the laughter of two men playing cards.

After helping clean up the lunch mess, Mac and Cheese walked Lucy and Milo to the back fence.

"About that Purple Heart you found. We keep some records of the men who come through if they want to leave a forwarding address. Sometimes they identify their unit and batallion, like the Dirty Thirty. You're welcome to them," Cheese said. "You can also check with the Veterans of Foreign Wars and the American Legion to see if they are familiar with the Dirty Thirty. Not sure how helpful they'll be, as some can be a little prickly about Vietnam veterans. But it's worth a try. It sure would be nice to get that medal and those pictures home."

Lucy looked at Milo. She thought about her dad, wondering suddenly if he had a Purple Heart and where it might be. And if he hadn't made it home, would she have wanted it? Would it have made her sad? Or grateful?

"Those kids?" Milo said, as if reading her thoughts. "They'll be wanting their dad's Purple Heart."

"How do you know? What if it's an awful reminder of something they don't want to think about? What if there was a good reason all that stuff got buried?" Lucy said.

Lucy had watched the Vietnam Veterans Against the War march in Washington on television just a couple of months ago. She had watched those men toss their combat ribbons, uniforms and helmets onto the Capitol steps in anger and frustration. She would never forget the way some of them cried. How some of them named friends they had lost into a microphone before throwing those medals and ribbons over the fence President Nixon had built right there on the Capitol steps to keep them out.

Milo shrugged. "All I know is I'd want it."

It was too much. The stones around Lucy's heart locked in place. She didn't want to think about another family and what they might have lost.

"You tell your dad he's welcome," Mac said to Lucy. "And we have family meetings, too, on Saturdays, if you two ever want to come for that."

Mac and Cheese seemed nice enough, but Lucy didn't want her dad anywhere near this place.

Eventually, Lucy and Milo left with a promise to come back and look through their records. They were quiet as they walked back to Milo's house. Lucy kicked pinecones along the path, and Milo picked up a new stick and decapitated weeds. When they got to Mrs. Bartolo's garden gate, Milo invited her in to watch *As the World Turns*.

"You watch soap operas?" Lucy said, mystified. Her

mother would never let her watch a soap opera. They were pointless and had no educational value.

"No matter how bad things get, those people always have it worse. Plus, Grams makes popcorn with butter."

"No, thanks," Lucy said.

"Suit yourself."

Milo let himself through the gate and into the backyard. Then he turned around. "I'm going to find that family one way or another. Do you want to help me?"

Lucy's feelings were all over the place, so she wrangled them as best she could and concentrated on being reasonable. She heard her dad's reasonable voice in her head, guiding her. *We should always seek to be an instrument in this life.*

"I'll think about it," Lucy said. And meant it.

possibility

*L*ucy, Mom and Dad used to watch the Fourth of July fireworks from the top of their Chicago apartment building along with everyone else who lived there. The fireworks shot off from Soldier Field, and even though they weren't especially close, they had a perfect view between two other buildings. Dad was in charge of grilling hot dogs, and Mom would make Aunt Rosie's famous macaroni salad. Ernie from the third floor brought homemade root beer, and later on, when the dessert was eaten and the fireworks watched, all the kids would run around the rooftop painting fiery shapes against the dark of night with the tips of their sparklers.

It was one of Lucy's favorite days of the year.

This year, with the family party coming up next weekend, there were no plans for grilled hot dogs or homemade root beer. No one bought sparklers. Mom spent the day afraid of how Dad might react to the sound of distant fireworks, so Lucy worried, too.

At sundown, after pacing around the house most of the day, maybe afraid of his own reaction as well, Dad left out the sliding glass door to go for a walk. He didn't come back for hours.

Long after bedtime, when Lucy heard the door open and close again, she crept out to the family room. Mom and Dad sat on the sofa in a patch of moonlight, Mom's head on his shoulder. Lucy settled back into the shadows to watch.

"It isn't the explosions I was worried about," Dad said.

Mom reached for his hand and squeezed it.

Dad sighed. "After a long day, sometimes we'd go outside and lie on the roof of the barracks. We'd watch the live fire rounds go off into the sky, like fireworks. It was beautiful. People were dying, but the sky was beautiful."

Lucy watched her parents' secret moment and longed to be right between them, to feel them on either side, holding her together.

A bang went off in the distance. Bang. Bang. Both Mom and Dad startled, and the moment was broken.

———

Monday morning, Lucy got herself ready by spraying her Aqua Velva and counting her stones into her pockets, which were starting to fray at the seams. Her other two pairs of shorts were also showing some wear, and she packed them into a small bag so she could mend them with Aunt Rosie's sewing kit.

As she walked into the kitchen to grab a glass of orange juice on her way next door, she was surprised to find Dad sitting at the breakfast table, shaved, showered and wearing a blue suit and red tie. His hair was a bit wonky, but Lucy supposed it took some getting used to, combing your hair with one hand. Dad's empty sleeve was carefully folded and pinned under itself. Mom sat beside him sipping coffee.

"Where are you going?" Lucy pulled out her own chair.

"Stanford Hospital." Dad said. "I have a meeting with Dr. Wilson about their cardiology program. Or, more specifically, if I need to train in residency or if I can use the training I already have."

"So you won't have to go back to school?" Lucy said.

Mom took Dad's hand like she had last night. "Your dad was one of the top three surgeons in his program. It's why Stanford hired him before he left for the war. They'd be lucky to have him back, with or without the added training. He can learn as he goes."

"Of course they'd be lucky," Lucy said. She looked at the folded sleeve and wondered if it might be better to wear the prosthetic. Sort of like wearing your best suit, you should probably go to a job interview with all your limbs.

But Lucy did not point this out to her father. Not after their last conversation about his arm. Instead, Lucy looked back and forth between Mom and Dad while they chatted about the logistics of the day—how Dad would drive Mom to her first day of work and pick her up.

"It's okay. Richard can give me a ride home," Mom said. Richard was Mom's new boss. "They may want to take you out for cocktails, or dinner."

"I'll pick you up," Dad said.

"Really, it's no problem. Richard has offered to drive me home whenever you need the car."

"I'll pick you up!" Dad said again, with entirely too much gusto.

Mom went back to sipping coffee, her hand curled into a fist around the handle of the cup. After a couple of minutes, where the silence seemed to build itself up into what felt to Lucy like static electricity, Dad turned his attention to her.

"Giovanni said you've uncovered a mystery," he said.

Happy to change the subject, Lucy talked about the helmet, the pictures and the Purple Heart she'd found with Milo.

"Did you get one?" Lucy asked. "A Purple Heart?"

"I did. Our field commander came to the hospital and handed them out of a box." Dad looked her straight in the eye. "It's a worthy goal, Lucia. Returning something like that to the family."

"What if they don't want it?" Lucy said. "What if it just reminds them of something they've lost?"

She couldn't help but think of those men on the Capitol steps, the medals they'd earned getting thrown over the fence.

"What if they do want it? What if they've been looking for it? You can't know the answer until you take the steps to get there. To me, it's a medal of merit, a reminder of resilience and bravery," Dad finished.

Lucy thought of the men who came through Mac and Cheese's, some who'd left their families, homeless men she'd seen on the television news.

"Not everyone is resilient and brave," Lucy said.

"That is true," Dad said. "Sadly, that is very true."

Lucy studied the raised scar on Dad's chin from so long ago. "Can I see it? Your Purple Heart?"

"Of course."

Dad scooted back from the table and went around the corner into their bedroom. Lucy heard a dresser door open and close. He walked back out with a purple box and set it down in front of Lucy.

She opened the box and touched the heart-shaped medal, the profile of George Washington and his crest, the purple ribbon with the white edges. The pin in back of the ribbon meant for it to be fastened to a jacket or a shirt and worn with honor. She expected to feel proud of her father, of what he'd sacrificed, what they'd all sacrificed, so he could save lives. More lives, he'd told her in one of his letters, than he'd probably ever save once he got back home.

But instead of feeling proud or relieved or hopeful or elated, looking at that Purple Heart made her feel like she'd stepped off a curb somewhere and just missed getting hit by a bus. Because he could have died. And sometimes, when Lucy had gone too long without seeing him during the day, she'd start to worry she had the facts wrong. That maybe he had died. That his coming home without an arm was just a dream she'd wake from at any moment.

Mom took the box from her, ran her own thumb along the ridges of George Washington's face and then snapped it shut. She smiled at Lucy. "You also said this was important to Milo, right? Maybe this is a way you can be useful to your friend."

"I wouldn't say we're friends. We just met."

"Well, possibility, then. Do it for what might be possible, and what you might discover along the way," Dad said, reminding Lucy of Uncle G's definition of serendipity.

Dad stared at the purple box sitting next to a plate of buttered toast. "We are blessed, Lucia. Blessed that I am still here. This medal reminds me that I have a choice to make. Every day. We all do. To keep moving forward. A strong person knows this."

Lucy wondered if he was talking more to himself than to her. "I am a strong person," she said.

"Yes you are. You are my brave, strong girl. And if anyone can help Milo find the owner of that Purple Heart, it's you."

For the first time since he'd been home, it felt like a normal conversation, one that could have taken place before he left, and Lucy was hopeful that little by little, conversation by conversation, they'd get themselves back to where they used to be.

It was settled, then. Lucy would show Dad that she was, in fact, his brave, strong girl. That she could handle this journey of the Purple Heart, wherever it may lead her.

a flight of dragonflies

*a*fter phoning Milo, Lucy sat at the table with Uncle G, head in her hands, waiting for him to show up so they could get this whole thing started. Cannoli kept butting her head against her ankle until she picked her up into her lap.

"Whatcha thinking about?" Uncle G said. A novel was propped on the table beside his plate of toast, *Catch-22*, and he sipped black coffee out of a chipped mug that said DAD-O.

There had been times over the last year when Lucy was certain her worries would grow big enough to kill her. During those times, her mouth would pucker into a tight frown without her consent. When she caught herself, she tried to relax her jaw, her cheeks, her lips, but as soon as she stopped thinking about it, bang! The sixty-two frown muscles in her face had a mind of their own.

But instead of telling her that her face would freeze, as

the aunts often did, or calling her lemon-face, as the Joes always did, Uncle G would just let her sit there beside him on the sofa, quiet, frowning for all she was worth, and wouldn't say a thing. She knew her fears and worries and facial expressions were safe with Uncle G.

"I'm worried about Dad. He won't put on his arm."

"He won't put on his arm, huh? Well, that's not something you hear every day."

Uncle G smiled, trying to lighten her load, maybe. Lucy was used to it. Most adults thought she was too serious, too reasonable, too quiet. The aunts would even spit at her sometimes if they thought the evil eye was upon her, as though reasonableness were evil. Sometimes she'd find dried herbs stuffed into her drawers after the aunts had come for a visit.

"He roams around at night. I don't think he's sleeping. He loses his patience over tuna fish sandwiches."

Uncle G set the toast on his plate. "It's going to take some time, Lucy. He's only been home for three weeks."

"He's not himself." Lucy scratched behind Cannoli's ears, and she lightly bit her thumb with affection.

"Of course he's not. He may never be that self again. But that doesn't have to be a bad thing. We're always changing, all of us."

Just then, Aunt Rosie rounded the corner wearing elbow-length sunshine-yellow rubber gloves. She turned up the volume on the small television in the adjacent family room and then threw open the oven door, prepared to clean.

Before she got to work, she hollered, "Gia, come here this instant and pick up your shoes. They're next to the TV!"

"I'm writing a letter to President Nixon!" Gia yelled from her room.

"Why are you cleaning the oven?" Uncle G said. "It cleans itself."

"I don't trust anything to clean itself. Including you," Aunt Rosie said. Then she yelled, "I don't care if you're writing a letter to President Nixon, get out here and clean up your mess!"

"Stop yelling!" Uncle G yelled. He slammed his hand flat on the table. Which he was forever doing. An Uncle G exclamation point.

"Get off your *culo* and go tell her yourself, then," Aunt Rosie said from inside the oven. "I'm tired of always being the *mostro*."

Uncle G pushed back from the table and stomped around the corner and down the hallway toward Gia's room, yelling in Italian. Or maybe he was saying *fi, fie, fo, fum*, for all Lucy knew. Without her permission at all, she giggled.

Then Aunt Rosie giggled. Then Gia came out to fetch her shoes, saw them giggling, and giggled herself. It almost felt like old times. When they'd been like sisters.

Then the newscaster started talking about the Vietnam draft.

Gia sat down on the sofa, the plastic cover crunching beneath her weight, as the newscaster talked about the Vietnam draft lottery that would be airing next month. She balled her fists and punched the plastic seat, making a popping sound. "Jerks!"

"You're just making yourself more upset," Aunt Rosie said from beside the oven. Gia flipped off the television, stomped back to her room and slammed the door.

"Are we ever to have a peaceful meal in this house?" Uncle G roared as he sat back down at the breakfast table.

Aunt Rosie laid her yellow-gloved hand on his shoulder. "Josh is eighteen, Giovanni. His birth date will be in the lottery next month."

Uncle Giovanni swore quietly.

The news hit Lucy hard, like a shove to the chest, and she could hardly catch her breath. She wondered if there would ever be a time that bad news didn't feel that way, if she was forever doomed to live her life as a clenched fist of worry.

————

Milo knocked on Uncle G's door at ten o'clock sharp. He had a shovel slung over one shoulder and his overstuffed rucksack slung over the other. With his uniform—cutoff jean shorts, giant red T-shirt and black Converse—in place, Lucy wondered if he'd brought any other clothes with him from North Carolina.

"You're digging a hole, not moving to Argentina," Lucy said.

"Speak for yourself."

Milo seemed in a mood. The way Uncle G could get sometimes. Like a bear, all pinch-faced and growling and claws ready to scratch. She wondered if Milo's moods passed the way Uncle G's did, like summer storms.

Lucy sighed and followed him toward the creek. "Whoever buried that Purple Heart did it on purpose. Don't you feel like we're about to rob a grave?"

Milo stopped in his tracks and looked at Lucy. Hard. "I feel like we're doing something that needs to be done. If you don't want to, that's up to you. But stop chattering about it."

Which Lucy supposed was fair. And her father was right; they wouldn't know anything until they accomplished their task. "Well, you don't have to act so annoyed about it. I'm entitled to my feelings."

Milo kept walking.

There were a few dragonflies flitting above the sun-dappled creek and Lucy took a moment to get her bearings, looking up through the canopy of trees she'd identified with the tree catalog from Great-Uncle Lando's nursery. There were the snowflake-shaped leaves of the bigleaf maple, the bushy white alders and western sycamores. Here and there were coastal live oaks, and the ferns that grew confident in all the shade. Birds sang harmony with the trickle of the creek as it moved around the stones that had been pushing through the earth for thousands of years. There was comfort for Lucy in knowing, precisely, how to identify everything.

Eventually, they both stood looking down at the wishing stone that marked the place where the helmet was buried. The dirt was still soft, so it didn't take long for Milo to dig it all up. He handed Lucy the helmet, and when Lucy lifted the flap of the lining, the pictures were there, but the Purple Heart was gone.

"Oh my gosh!" Lucy said, and fell to her knees to dig around in the hole. "The Purple Heart fell out!"

"I've got it," Milo said.

"What do you mean?" Lucy sat back on her heels and shaded her eyes from the sun. "How can you have it?"

"I never put it back, okay?"

Lucy just blinked at him.

"I think I was meant to find it."

Hold the fort. Now he sounded like Great-Aunt Lilliana with her irrational premonitions. Which never came true. Except for sometimes. Which was the scientific nature of things, anyway.

Then, as though the universe was conspiring against the scientific nature of things, the dragonflies came.

Green, yellow and blue, the sky was filled with iridescence and the soft whispering of wings. Milo laid the shovel down softly and raised his arms out to his sides. He closed his eyes and made soft clicking sounds as though trying to call them.

But much to Lucy's dismay, they came to her instead.

They landed on her arms, her shoulders and down the front of her shirt. Her first instinct was to run, screaming, but she held still, arms raised ever so slightly so she wouldn't squish them against her sides.

"It's a swarm!" she whispered, panicked, trying not to

move her mouth too much in case one might fly in. "What's happening?"

"It's called a flight. A flight of dragonflies," Milo said, mystified. "It doesn't happen very often, but it's nothing to worry over."

Which was not particularly comforting to Lucy. Eyes closed and concentrating, Milo seemed hopeful they'd land on him, too. He stood so still, Lucy wondered if he was breathing, but those flashing bits of iridescence ignored him. And even though Lucy was slightly annoyed that Milo had swiped the Purple Heart without telling her, and still unsure if they should even be doing this in the first place, the sheer wonder of the moment, and Milo's obvious yearning for the flying insects, broke through her fear.

Lucy inched herself, ever so slowly, to stand right beside him. She raised her arm to his and took his hand, hoping the dragonflies might see how much he seemed to need and want them. She waved her other arm so they might dislodge themselves and find a better, steadier place to land.

Her plan worked.

Little by little, the dragonflies lifted from her arms, shoulders and head, and flutter-buzzed straight for Milo. They dotted his shirt, his ears, his spiky blond hair. One even landed on the top curve of his glasses. Lucy watched as a wide smile took over his face.

He said, softly, "My dad and me. We would draw them into our sketchbooks. But only the ones we saw up close and personal. Then we would compare the drawings to the book we have with all the different species and their names.

"My dad . . ." Milo said. It took him a few moments to go on. "He's in Vietnam."

Lucy blinked. "What?"

"He's career military. We've lived at Fort Bragg for the last three years."

Thinking back over her time with Milo, Lucy supposed it made perfect sense. "Was that why you wanted to see my dad come home?"

Milo nodded, and a handful of dragonflies flew away.

She had never met another kid with a dad in the war. "When does he come home?"

Milo hesitated again. "Forty days."

Because her dad had come home almost three months early, Lucy imagined it only got harder as that homecoming day approached. Time stretched when waiting for the best of things, like birthdays or Christmas. Waiting for a dad to come home was like waiting for every good thing that will ever happen, combined.

"This will help me pass the time," Milo said, holding on to the Purple Heart.

"My dad has one," Lucy said.

"I figured."

Lucy was glad he didn't ask about Dad's arm. She didn't want to talk about it. Probably the same way he didn't want to talk about his own dad; otherwise, he would have already. She thought about Tabitha, Rubin and Trina back in Chicago, how sometimes, on a bad day, quiet togetherness was just as important as laughing on a good day. How friendship was just as much about what you said to each other as what you didn't.

She'd gone a long time without a friend.

Eventually, one by one, the dragonflies had better places to be. They fluttered here and there in between the leaves and low against the water, like fairy sprites. And in all the commotion and chaos of her life, all the uncertainty that seemed to just keep coming, Lucy was overcome by a feeling of momentary peace. She would never look at dragonflies the same way again. They were forever tied to Milo.

"I think you found your talent, even if it is mostly useless." Milo grinned, looking after the dragonflies. "Thank you."

Lucy thought about her friendless year. How she'd look across the school yard at the clumps of girls laughing so easily with each other, touching each other's hair or blowing dandelions together, sharing their secret wishes. She knew that was something she wanted, with an unexpected feeling of desperation, but didn't know how to achieve. Because her attempts at talking to the Dandelion Girls—*did you know the word* dandelion *comes from the French* dent de lion, *which means "lion's tooth," because that's what the leaves look like?*—had made her feel strange, as though she were a clumsy giant plodding through their fairy kingdom. The way they'd looked at her. Especially Linda McCollam.

So Lucy had gathered it up, all her feelings of hurt and loneliness, and pressed them down and down where they cooked and crushed like igneous rocks deep inside the earth. Easy peasy. Instead of trying again, and maybe again, she went to the library, where the facts she read about didn't look at her funny or whisper to each other behind her back. But those facts didn't listen to her sadness, either, or keep good company.

Maybe it was time for Lucy to think about what came next.

cans and string

grandma Miller called every Wednesday night—rain or shine, through sickness and in health—at seven o'clock sharp. It was the only evening during the week that Grandma wasn't otherwise engaged, or so she said. No bridge, no volunteering for the Junior League. No teas, garden parties or quilting groups. Wednesday was Grandma's "Me" day, and she'd often remind Mom and Lucy of it. They were lucky, she'd said many times, that she found time to call them at all.

And every Wednesday night, Lucy prepared herself for Grandma's nonstop talking. Grandma didn't believe in question marks.

Your last letter could have used better penmanship. I won three penmanship awards when I was your age. Schools these days are not what they used to be.

Your mother tells me you aren't starting with the Junior

League until the fall. That is a bit late. Most girls are well under way by junior high school.

I've sent a packet of seeds for your garden. Zinnias. Every garden needs zinnias.

By the time Lucy would hand the phone over to Mom, Lucy felt as though she'd been poked repeatedly with a sharp stick.

This Wednesday was no different.

"We'll be there on Saturday, of course. I assume there is much to do for your father's party, and we want to be helpful. Don't force your mother to remind you to get a bag ready. We aren't leaving without you. Grandpa and I simply won't take no for an answer."

Lucy tried to tell Grandma that she was in the process of making a friend. That she was also involved in an important task. Maybe even a heroic task, depending on the outcome. Lucy wondered if they might even get their names in the papers.

KIDS REUNITE PURPLE HEART WITH WOUNDED WARRIOR!

It was possible, anyway. But Grandma, as usual, wasn't listening. Except to herself.

When Lucy finally handed the phone back to Mom, relieved that it was over, Dad said, "You should go. You know how much Grandpa wants to take you fishing."

He sat at their small dining room table next to a pile of reference books on blood disease. The table was a rattan upgrade Mom had brought home from the apartment complex. They were remodeling the clubhouse.

Lucy couldn't imagine leaving, couldn't imagine spending one more minute away from her father. She was heartbroken he didn't feel the same way. So heartbroken, she couldn't find the words to respond.

Later, Mom and Dad were in their room whisper-fighting about it, Dad insisting Lucy would be better off sent away. At least for a little while.

"She's watching you, Anthony. She's watching every choice you make right now."

"That's my point! I don't want her following me around, watching me. I can't think straight."

"What will that say to her, if you send her away?"

While Lucy tried not to listen, she laid out the three photos from inside the helmet on her nightstand: the man and the little girl, the girl and the boy, and the blustery-haired woman. All three were taken at the beach, on a blanket spread out across the sand. The picture of the man and the little girl had names written on the back: *Johnny and Amanda, 1963*.

Had Johnny come back home and buried his helmet and his family? Did that mean he'd left them? Or had he died and someone else did it for him?

And if he had left his family, what was the final straw?

A wife who fought with him?

A daughter who followed him around too much?

Lucy wanted to gather as much information as she could

so she would understand what to watch for in her father, what sorts of things might drive a person right over the edge. Then, at least, she would know what not to do.

By Thursday, Lucy was caught up in Rossi family pandemonium. With Dad's Welcome Home party this weekend, everyone was going crazy making food and plans. And even though there had been no word on Stanford Hospital, Dad seemed optimistic, while also compiling a list of other possibilities, so Lucy felt that way, too. At least about his job prospects.

Lucy and Milo also came up with a plan. Milo sketched multiple copies of the insignia for the Dirty Thirty, and they decided to ride their bikes to the Veterans of Foreign Wars and the American Legion. In both places, they would explain what they had found and what they were trying to do. Lucy suggested they go to the city library and see Ms. Lula, since she had access to more information than President Nixon.

Lucy had asked Uncle G about Milo. He informed her that Milo was an only child and that his mom was working back in North Carolina. That usually she came during the summer for a visit with Milo, but not this summer. He told her that Milo was staying through August, as his family thought it might be nice for him to have a change of scene, a vacation of sorts.

"Why didn't you tell me his dad was in Vietnam?"

Uncle G smoothed back his wavy hair. "If Milo wants to talk about his personal life with you, then he can. It's not my story to tell."

Which was true, but also extraordinarily frustrating.

It seemed Uncle G knew something Lucy didn't.

On Friday, Lucy and Milo were set to visit the American Legion, but one of the Joes got sick with food poisoning, so it was up to Lucy to fill in his meatball delivery schedule. When she told Milo they'd have to go later in the day, he asked to help. That way they could finish in half the time because Lucy wouldn't have to go back to the deli for a second round.

Because most of her family would be in and out of the deli preparing food for Dad's party, she worried, of course, that Milo would take one look at the more colorful members of her family and she'd never see him again. Besides losing the only friend she'd been able to make in San Jose, he'd go about the Purple Heart mission without her, and then she'd have no way of proving to her dad she was still his brave, strong girl.

Lucy tried to suggest that they meet after she was finished with her work, but Milo wasn't having it. He wanted to meet the rest of her family. She reluctantly agreed.

When she rode her bike over to pick him up, Mrs. Bartolo was on the porch, holding a ladder in place. Milo hung a hummingbird feeder, its bright pink liquid sloshing.

"I don't know what I'd have done without Milo this

summer," Mrs. Bartolo said to Lucy as she walked up with her bike. "It seems like everything is falling apart at once."

"Grams, you're the one who taught me how to do all this stuff."

"Yes, but it's nicer to drink lemonade and watch someone else do it," Mrs. Bartolo said, and snort-laughed.

As they rode their bikes from Mrs. Bartolo's to the Pink Kitchen Deli, all Lucy could think about was the Frank Sinatra music that would be blaring and the gilt-framed photo of the Pope and Nonnina's urn. So by the time they stopped in front of the bright pink building that was the same bright pink as Papo Angelo's kitchen at home, which he had never changed from Nonnina's original design—and declared he never would so long as he was in his right mind and free from drooling—Lucy was ready to fall over from pure thinking-exhaustion and anticipated embarrassment.

"It's like Pepto-Bismol," Milo said with wonder.

"I should warn you . . ." Lucy said, but had absolutely no idea what else to say that might prepare Milo for the rest of her family, so she didn't say anything at all.

Great-Aunt Lilliana and the other two Belly Button Aunts—Ida and Florence—were Papo Angelo's sisters. Each aunt wore a white butcher's apron, her hair pinned up in a net. They spoke Italian, cackling and laying fresh dough out on white bedsheets as Lucy and Milo walked in. Papo Angelo stood behind the counter running prosciutto through the meat slicer with his thick hands. He wore a shower cap, insisting it was far more hygienic than hairnets.

"Why are you slicing prosciutto instead of helping?" yelled Great-Aunt Lilliana to Papo, motioning to the crank machine she was using to flatten the dough. "My shoulder isn't getting any younger!"

"You rather slice the prosciutto, sis?"

"Lucia! Grab a couple of hairnets!" Great-Aunt Lilliana threw her hand in the air, her large diamond ring sparkling. When Lucy and Milo didn't move quickly enough, she went on. "Why are you two just standing there like a couple of yokels?" She pointed at Lucy with one crooked finger. "You. Go fetch me another bag of flour. And you"—she pointed to Milo—"grab the cooler in the back and load six packs of meatballs from the freezer. Plus bring me some eggs. Chop-chop." Great-Aunt Lilliana clapped her hands, sending a puff of flour into the air.

"Not hairnets, shower caps!" Papo Angelo reminded everyone.

"His name is Milo, for the record," Lucy said to no one in particular.

Lucy and Milo tucked their hair into shower caps, Lucy's blue, Milo's green, both clearly marked HARRAH'S RENO from Papo's last gambling trip. Lucy then led Milo to the back room and handed him the cooler they used for deliveries. Next, she took him into the walk-in freezer stocked with meatballs and all the other packaged meat Papo had gotten on his last meat run. Stock was running low.

"Sorry about this," Lucy said, meaning the shower caps, but ended up gesturing to everything.

"Who's that?" Milo asked, pointing to a large portrait of Nonnina that hung on the freezer wall.

"That's my grandma. Papo likes to hang her picture everywhere. He's afraid he'll forget what she looks like. She died two years ago."

Milo nodded, looking serious. "She has very red hair."

Which was true. Nonnina used to get her hair dyed every month by a lady named Vera, who wore hotpants. The aunts used to cluck about it at family gatherings as though it was a tragedy, like *Romeo and Juliet*, only with hair. Although whether they meant the red hair or Vera's hotpants, Lucy was never sure.

They hurried back out, and Milo set the cooler on the pink Formica table next to the refrigerated case of sliced lunch meat and salads. Lucy showed Milo how to stack the meatballs in the coolers. Then they went outside to attach the coolers to the handlebars of their bikes with Papo Angelo's bungee cords.

When they went back inside for the list of deliveries, Great-Aunt Lilliana spied Milo up and down. "You're Italian."

It wasn't a question. Since Great-Aunt Lilliana was Fattucchiera, she thought she knew everything. She was the reason Lucy feared tomatoes and chanting.

"Nope," Milo said.

"Bah. On your father's side. There is someone."

Great-Aunts Ida and Florence made *tsk*ing sounds as they pressed the dough into circles, which would eventually be deep-fried and stuffed with cannoli filling. The aunts were tiny, fluttery like birds, and all the children in the family usually grew taller than the aunts by the time they hit ten years old. No one teased them, though, or they might find a chicken foot in their soup or worse. Their lunch box.

"Aunt Lilliana," Lucy said, "not everyone is Italian. Plus, he has blond hair."

"Northern Italians have blond hair. Your aunt Catarina had blond hair, may she rest in peace."

"Well, now that that's out of the way," Papo Angelo said. "Don't worry. We'll make you an honorary Italian, Milo. You just have to pass the test." Then he rang the Alaska bell beside the cash register for no reason whatsoever. Normally, he only ever rang that bell when someone tipped him. He'd been saving tip money since before Nonnina died for an Alaskan cruise she'd always wanted to go on. He claimed he was still planning on taking her, no matter when that day came.

"What test?" Lucy said. This was news to her, and she panicked, sure she wouldn't pass because she had so much Miller in her. But then Uncle G, Gia and Josh came in the front door to start making the Italian sausage and distracted everyone. Uncle G kissed his first two fingers and placed them on the gilt frame of the giant picture of Nonnina that hung next to John F. Kennedy and Giovanni Battista Enrico Antonio Maria Montini, otherwise known as the Pope.

Great-Aunt Lilliana smacked Uncle G on the shoulder. "You here to be a scoundrel?" she said.

Uncle G winked. "Always."

"I'm not wearing a hairnet or a shower cap, just so we're

clear," Gia said, and flopped herself down in one of the chairs, flinging her hair over her shoulder. Josh good-naturedly reached for a shower cap and pretended to tuck his buzzed-short hair underneath. He crossed his eyes at Lucy, and she feared her heart might race itself to death. His hazel eyes. His tanned arms and wide shoulders. Her physical reaction was baffling. Or maybe it was pheromones. Lucy had read that humans secrete chemicals in their sweat that other humans can sense and are attracted to, like bees to honey. It was all disgusting and mysterious, but she was at a loss as to what else could be happening to her.

All three aunts stopped what they were doing and stared at Gia. She sighed, grabbing a hairnet out of the basket. Since she had blow-dried her curly hair straight, she was having a tough time shoving it all into the hairnet. "Doesn't anyone respect the child labor laws in this family? You should at least let us unionize, right, Lucy?"

Gia was obsessed with politics. Lucy didn't remember the last time they'd had a conversation about anything else. She missed her cousin.

On his way to grab a biscotti out of the tin on the counter, Josh tugged Lucy's right braid and winked as though he knew what she might be thinking.

Lucy wondered how Josh felt about the upcoming draft lottery. Nervous, probably, but would he go to Vietnam? Or would he be one of those conscientious objectors? Would he go to Canada? Would he burn his draft card so that he'd always be on the run from the law? Was he willing to go to prison for his beliefs? Lucy knew how Gia felt, about everything, whether she wanted to or not, but not Josh. She only knew he'd played football, wanted to be a veterinarian and was the irrational love of her life.

As if there wasn't enough going on, Papo turned on the music and "North to Alaska" blared over the speakers Nonnina had put up in the corners of the deli.

Uncle G twirled Great-Aunt Lilliana around the table, the other aunts tapping their feet to the country-western tune. Josh twirled Gia, and Lucy wished it could have been her. She wondered sometimes if all her family was connected with invisible string, the kind connecting one can to another like an old-fashioned walkie-talkie. Except her. When the music blasted, everyone danced, while Lucy preferred to watch.

"Your family is very . . ." Milo said, his eyes wide open. "Enthusiastic."

Lucy wondered what they must look like from the outside, dancing around in shower caps and hairnets, and sighed. Why did her family have to be so peculiar? Why couldn't they be more respectable, like the Millers? Photographs in the freezer. Aunts who tried to heal the flu with a tomato. Grandmothers in brass urns. It was all too much. Even if she had tried to make friends last year, one look at this family, and they would have scattered like cockroaches under a too-bright light.

She half wondered what might be wrong with Milo that he didn't scatter, too.

Great-Aunt Lilliana handed Lucy a bouquet of flowers.

"But it's only Thursday," Lucy said.

"And we're going to be at your father's party on Sunday when Joe usually takes them. What? You don't want your uncle Ralph to have his flowers? You don't want Big Papo or Big Nona to have theirs?"

Great-Aunts Ida and Florence both stopped what they were doing and looked at Lucy, which made her worry about chicken feet.

"Of course not," Lucy said. "I just don't like cemeteries."

"Bah," Aunt Ida said. "It's the only place where no one talks back!"

Great-Aunts Ida and Florence both cackled while Great-Aunt Lilliana said, "Except ungrateful nieces." Then she turned to Milo. "It will be tough. But you can do it."

Which was Great-Aunt Lilliana being Fattucchiera again, thinking she knew something when she didn't. Either that, or Uncle G had told her Milo's dad was in Vietnam, so she was taking a wild guess at how he might feel about cemeteries at the moment.

Great-Aunt Lilliana cupped Milo's chin in her hand and gave him one of her tight Fattucchiera hugs. The kind that usually meant *prepare for the worst*.

"Now, *andare avanti*! Get going!" Great-Aunt Lilliana said, wiping at the corner of her eye.

Oh, good gracious. If Milo stuck around after all this, he deserved a prize.

"Here's to Alaska!" Papo Angelo said while he wiped at

the small glass cabinet that held Nonnina's urn. A plain brass urn that Nonnina had picked out at a garage sale as a joke one day. *When I'm dead, I don't want anything fancy. Just stick me in this pot and take me with you everywhere.*

Trouble was, that's just what Papo Angelo did.

This family, a bunch of cans and string tied together.

everything else in the universe

*L*ucy attempted to distract Milo with funny stories about her family so they might not seem so crazy. She talked about all manner of things while they rode from house to house delivering meatballs, keeping up a constant chatter. Like how Great-Uncle Lando had bought a box of New Year's Eve supplies off the back of some guy's truck at a deep discount because it was July. Blow horns and clackers and bags of exploding confetti. There were even a bunch of HAPPY NEW YEAR tinsel tiaras that he was especially proud of and couldn't wait to make everyone wear at Dad's party.

That was when she realized funny and crazy were two shades of the same color, like burgundy and red, and so she stopped talking about her family altogether.

"Your uncle G invited me to your dad's party," Milo said.

"Believe me, you don't want to come. There's going to be too many people, which means a lot of yelling. Plus, they'll make you work filling champagne glasses or mixing the antipasto salad or worse."

"Worse like what? Removing bodies in the dead of night?"

"Ha."

"I'd like to come. Uncle G invited Grams, too."

If Lucy could have fallen over and died, she would have. Dead meant she wouldn't have to suffer any more embarrassment at the hands of her family. Plus, how much was too much for Milo?

The Pink Kitchen Deli activities were one thing, the Family Gathering activities were something else entirely. The Belly Button Aunts would bring their pouches of herbs, and Great-Aunt Lilliana would announce her premonitions, and then there was the way her family ate polenta and how many courses there were so that if you stuffed yourself with too much ravioli or *sugo* meat, you wouldn't have enough room for the pork butt and roasted peppers and then the Belly Button Aunts might think you were sick and insist on lighting a candle to the saints for your health. Then there was always the pinochle and the fistfights.

Nonnina's urn would have its own chair next to Papo.

"Suit yourself, I guess." Lucy felt her face tense up the way it had while Dad had been gone.

After an hour of deliveries—all commenced while chasing an escaped dog, holding a crying baby while Mrs. Frank looked for change and drinking endless glasses of lemonade—Lucy decided they'd earned their lunch and the two dollars in tips they'd been given. Lucy was hot, damp from sweat and hungry as she led the way down Madden Avenue and stopped in front of the Calvary Catholic Cemetery, her sunhat flopping.

"You stay here. I'll just drop off the flowers, and I'll be out in five minutes," Lucy said, trying to be sensitive to the fact that Milo might not want to be reminded that people, in fact, die.

Instead, Milo grabbed his rucksack and marched toward the cemetery gates like he was facing down death itself. Lucy followed with the bouquet Great-Aunt Lilliana had given her.

Big Nona's headstone was carved with China roses, the kind Big Papo had grown because they meant grace and lasting beauty. Big Papo's was right beside hers. They'd died within two months of each other, their hearts so intertwined, Great-Aunt Lilliana had said, they couldn't live one without the other. There were a few more Rossi family headstones that stood side by side in the shade of two sycamores. Milo sat on the grass right between them, elbows on knees, chin in his hands.

"It's nice here," he said. "The grass looks like carpet."

Lucy nodded, taking her sunhat off and running a hand across her sweaty forehead. "Mr. Jefferson keeps things tidy. I've seen him on his hands and knees, even, trimming around the headstones. He's obsessed with grass. Don't get him started, or he'll talk forever."

"You've got to have pride in what you do. No matter what you do. That's what my dad says."

"That's a fact," Lucy said.

Lucy handed him his meatball sandwich and offered him a bottle of RC Cola. Just then, a brilliant blue dragonfly touched down on the cap of the bottle.

"They're everywhere," Lucy said.

"Only in the summer. And only in certain climates. Dragonflies like it here," Milo said. The dragonfly hovered and then sped away. "She's a beautiful specimen. Did you know that Sikorsky, which designs helicopters, used a dragonfly wing as a model?"

"I did not know that."

"They used two thousand different drawings on an IBM computer and came up with the perfect wing."

"How do you know it's a she?"

Milo took out his sketchbook and flipped through, stopping on a page with several detailed pencil drawings of dragonflies. He pointed to the rounded edges at the bottom of one set of wings, and the S-curved edges at the bottom of another set. "The rounded ones are female."

A breeze lifted the edges of Milo's book, and Lucy glimpsed shimmering colors, just like the wings of the dragonflies. "Can I look?"

He handed it to her, and she flipped the pages slowly. Notes and pencil sketches of different parts of the dragonfly. Wings and abdomens, eyes and tails. Toward the back were watercolors, different species that looked like they'd been plucked from a dream, with soft edges and colors. They sparkled and shined with iridescence, just like the real live things.

"How did you do that?" Lucy said.

Milo chewed a bite of sandwich. "I use mica chips. I crush them with a rock and add it to the paint."

"Mica is almost a three on the Moh's scale of mineral hardness," Lucy said.

If Milo found that a strange observation, he didn't say so.

"Sometimes I cheat and buy eye shadow. Wish I had a camera for the looks on people's faces at the drugstore. Sometimes they'll say, 'What a nice kid, buying eye shadow for your mom.' And I'll say, 'Nope, it's for me,' and let them think what they want."

He laughed and stuck Lucy's floppy hat on his own head, which then made her laugh. She touched the thick paper and read their names. *Seaside Dragonlet, Gray Petaltail, Vivid Dancer.*

Golden-winged Skimmer.

She looked carefully at the red dragonfly, the way its wings were darkest near the body and became lighter and lighter until the farthest tips of the wings were invisible, like the flames of a fire. Beyond the invisible tips of the wings were the lightest of swerving lines meant to look like heat, maybe. At least that was how it looked to Lucy.

"Where did you see it? The golden-winged skimmer?"

Milo pressed his lips together. "Just before I left Fayetteville. Cross Creek feeds into the Cape Fear River, and there's this perfect place for dragonflies. So I'd just take a folding chair out there sometimes and sketch for hours. I'd send Dad my sketches in letters. Sometimes he'd send back his own. But he's a terrible drawer, so they were mostly meant to be funny."

Milo reached in his back pocket and took out a tightly folded square of paper, unfolded it and handed it to Lucy.

Lucy smiled. It was a cartoon sketch of a dragonfly with pointy wings and googly eyes. There was a line drawn to each part and labeled by name: *googly eyes*, *beer belly*, *bbq ribs*, *spindly legs*.

The line that pointed to the wing said *Grandpa Bud*.

Milo looked over her shoulder. "Grams says the wings of a dragonfly carry the souls of the departed. Grandpa Bud was my grandpa and we'd tease her about it sometimes, that Grandpa Bud was probably having the time of his life flying around with the dragonflies. She's pretty superstitious."

Lucy snorted. "No wonder she likes my family."

They sat together, quiet for a little while. Listening to the water burble in the fountain, and watching the zigging and zagging dragonflies, Lucy was overcome with a sense of homeostasis.

Later, as they gathered their trash and packed up to leave, Milo said, "You're lucky."

"Lucky?"

"To have such a big family. I just have Grams. Mom's an only child, and Dad grew up in a boys' home in Iowa. Grams has a brother in Florida, Uncle Sticks, but that's it."

"I think you're the lucky one," Lucy said. "When I'm around my family, I always feel like I'm waiting for something to explode. Champagne bottles. Ravioli. Tempers."

"I can see that," Milo said. "But I still think you're the lucky one."

Just then, the brilliant blue dragonfly caught in her peripheral vision. It hovered above Noona Peterson's headstone, just to the left of Big Papo's. Lucy read the inscription as she had so many times before:

> When we try to pick out anything by itself,
> we find it hitched
> to everything else in the universe.
> —John Muir

Those words always put a picture in Lucy's mind: a night sky with shimmering threads connecting stars into constellations. She thought again about her family. How they all seemed connected by invisible string. All but her. She wanted desperately to feel those connections, to know she belonged. But didn't know how to get there.

She was lucky, she supposed, just like Milo said. Her family might be a circus, but they were her circus. And even if she didn't quite feel connected, she wasn't sure what she'd do without them.

the american legion

*L*ucy and Milo rode their bikes from the Calvary Catholic Cemetery to the American Legion Auxiliary post. She turned her face up to the sun and took in the warmth. She really did love San Jose, every bit as much as she'd loved Chicago, even though she'd never admit it. Because where Chicago was an orderly series of blocks and buildings and street names, the L running through it all connecting the dots, San Jose was the opposite. There was no rhyme or reason that Lucy had been able to figure out. In some places, there were blocks of storefronts like the Pink Kitchen Deli and Dan's Electronics, Pop's Cleaners and Little B's Market. But then there were blocks of strawberry and sweet-corn fields where vendors sold their fruit and vegetables right on the newly poured sidewalks, two different freeways just around the corner. There were apartment complexes and cookie-cutter houses, and just up McKee Road was the Alum

Rock Park wilderness where, at the turn of the century, there had been a health spa and mineral bath with a dance hall, an aviary and a zoo.

San Jose was a circus. Just like her family.

"Is this right?" Milo said. "It looks like someone's house."

Which was true. The American Legion building was just a long brown ranch-style house with a brick chimney up the side.

Lucy double-checked the address Mac had given her. "That's what it says."

Milo shrugged and led the way.

As soon as they hit the porch, they knew they'd found the right place. Just outside the door was a plaque that read:

> *In the spirit of Service, Not Self, the mission of the American Legion Auxiliary is to support The American Legion and to honor the sacrifice of those who serve by enhancing the lives of our veterans, military and their families, both at home and abroad.*

Milo knocked on the door, but no one answered. Lucy could hear murmuring voices on the other side, so she shrugged at Milo and opened the door for herself. The smell hit her first: beer and cigarettes.

Inside to the left, where the living room should have been, was a wide-open space and a bar. There were two poles attached to the wall, one flying an American flag, the other a deep blue with the American Legion symbol in the middle.

An older man sat at the wooden bar hunched over a half-empty glass of beer; another man stood behind the bar polishing a silver shaker. To the right of the entryway was a meeting room of sorts with three round tables and folding chairs stacked against the wood-paneled wall in the corner.

"What can I do for you?" the man behind the bar asked. He had receding brown hair and brown eyes, a wide nose and a straight line for a mouth. He was so ordinary-looking, his features sliding into each other without the slightest fanfare, that Lucy was sure she'd forget his face as soon as she looked away. Just like the people on television commercials.

"A couple of veterans we know sent us your way," Milo said. He dug around in his rucksack and took out the sketch. "We found this helmet buried near Penitencia Creek and were told that's a symbol of the Dirty Thirty, first airmen to serve in Vietnam. We hoped you might have some in your member- ship. Or at least someone who might know someone."

"If you have a bulletin board, we thought we could leave the sketch up," Lucy said.

The barman turned his forgettable eyes toward Lucy. "Is that so?"

"There were some pictures with the helmet. And a Purple Heart. We'd like to reunite them with the family," Lucy said.

"Did you hear that, Louis? They want us to help."

Louis had a thin layer of hair over the top of his other- wise bald head. His nose was large and red and covered in purple veins. "We don't allow Vietnam veterans at this post," he said.

"What do you mean?" Lucy said.

"We don't want 'em here," the forgettable man said.

Lucy's mouth popped open, and she looked at Milo. "Why?" she said.

"They're a bunch of drug addicts. Unpatriotic bums. You watch the news, you'll see what I mean," the forgettable man said. "You're just kids. You wouldn't know."

Milo balled his fists, clenched his jaw. Lucy wondered if he might start to shake the way Dad had when he stepped off the plane. She reached out to put a hand on his arm, the way she'd seen Uncle G do so many times as a means of comfort. Then she turned back to the men.

"For your information, Milo's dad is serving in Vietnam, and my dad just got home," Lucy said. "The sign outside says you're supposed to be concerned with enhancing the lives of servicemen and their families. SERVICEMEN and their FAMILIES."

The two men looked at each other, raised eyebrows, probably not expecting Lucy's outburst.

"What makes you better than my dad?" Milo said. "This was his second tour. He's been in the army since he turned eighteen. He learned how to fly a chopper so he could risk his life every day to save the lives of other men. What did you do, huh?"

Louis's back went straight as he turned in his stool to face Milo. There were stains on the old man's T-shirt. "I was on the beach at Normandy. Ask your daddy what that means."

"I can't," Milo said. "Lucy just told you. He's in Vietnam."

Louis's face softened the smallest bit. Or it could have been Lucy's imagination. "Go on, now. You aren't going to find any help here."

Lucy was outraged and humiliated. "You should be ashamed of yourselves," was all she managed, even though she wanted to say a whole lot more. Including swears.

"You know who should be ashamed of themselves?" The barman suddenly raised his voice.

"That's enough, Lloyd. They're just kids," Louis said.

Lloyd slammed down the silver shaker he'd been holding. "You ask your dad about all those innocent lives over there. You ask him about the fragmentation bombs and the napalm."

"Best you go now," Louis said.

Milo stormed off, then turned at the door. "At least my dad didn't blow up a bunch of babies in Hiroshima and Nagasaki!"

Lucy ran to catch up as Milo slammed outside. "Wait!"

Milo paced back and forth in front of his bike, then stopped. "What about the next address?"

"What?"

"The next address. The Veterans of Foreign Wars. We need to go there, too."

"Milo, I don't think—"

"We need to go!"

Milo hopped on his bike and pedaled off in the wrong direction.

"You're going the wrong way! Just . . . follow me."

Lucy climbed on her bike, unsteady. She'd had no idea other veterans felt that way. And if this was how veterans of other wars felt about Vietnam, then why did Mac and Cheese send them there in the first place? Lucy felt herself go all jangly again, her earlier sense of homeostasis completely gone.

Onetwothreefourfive-sixseveneightnineten.

Milo looked like a bull ready to charge. If he could have stomped his foot and stabbed someone with his horns, he would have.

"Why do you want to go there? What if the same thing happens?"

"It's important to know who's on your side and who isn't," Milo said.

As Lucy pedaled, passing several of the houses where they'd delivered that day, waving to the small children she knew in their yards, Lucy dared to hope that things might be different at the Veterans of Foreign Wars.

It was not different.

They were nicer about it, but they didn't let Lucy and Milo hang their sign.

By the time Milo walked down the cracked front steps of the VFW, he was eerily still and quiet, like an unexploded bomb. Then he threw his bike to the ground, picked it up and threw it down again. One of the bungee cords snapped, and the empty meatball cooler dropped onto the grass. He kicked it like a football.

Without a word, Milo got onto his bike and pedaled away, his big red T-shirt billowing out behind him.

"Milo, I can't take both . . ." Lucy called after him.

But he never even slowed down.

ten thousand things

*b*ecause Lucy was a whiz at bungees, she was able to strap the two coolers one on top of the other. She had to pedal slowly, and avoid all the potholes and bumps along the way, as well as peer around the side of the whole contraption because it was too tall to see over. It took forever.

Lucy tried not to be mad at Milo. He'd clearly had an emotional breakdown. She fully understood why such a thing had occurred. But he'd also left her behind—left her alone to manage bungee cords and meatball coolers and then her family once she got back to the Pink Kitchen Deli—so she couldn't help herself.

While Lucy had been gone, Gia had put up flyers all over the front windows of the deli:

PICNIC FOR PEACE! SATURDAY, SEPT 4
HAPPY HOLLOW PARK

7:00 PM
COME DANCE UNDER THE STARS
LET THE POWER OF LOVE
OVERCOME
THE LOVE OF POWER!

"Dad's just finishing up at work, and he'll give us a ride home," Gia said when Lucy walked in. The rest of her family had gone. "Oh, and you missed it!"

"What?"

"Papo got the last dollar he needed for his trip to Alaska!"

Papo was busy behind the counter, wrapping up the last of the Italian sausages in their freezer bags. "To Alaska!" he shouted, and rang the bell a bunch of times. Josh raised both fists in the air in solidarity.

"But we weren't even open" was all Lucy could say, heartbroken to have missed such an event.

"Papo let in Mrs. Bartolo for a chat, and she insisted on paying for some cannoli. When she dropped a dollar into the tip jar, Papo rang the bell and announced that was it! The final dollar for his trip to Alaska. So then he gave the cannoli to Mrs. Bartolo for free after all. It was worth the hairnet, let me tell you," Gia said.

Lucy was suddenly overcome with feelings of pent-up anger, frustration and sadness. She'd done everything she was told, whether she wanted to or not, since moving to San Jose. She'd delivered meatballs, spent time at Uncle G's when she wanted to be home, talked to her grandma every single

Wednesday night and never complained about any of it. Gia never helped. With anything. And when she did, she always whined about it. *I won't wear a hairnet! We should be paid fair wages! That's going to ruin my nail polish!*

Why did Gia get to see history being made while Lucy was out sweating in the sun delivering meatballs and being rejected by World War II veterans who should have known better than to be mean to children?

"It's not fair!" Lucy shouted into Gia's startled face.

Then she slammed out the heavy glass door and pedaled as fast as she could. Pedaled all the way home, even though Josh had called after her, and it was mostly uphill and only four o'clock, and Mom said Lucy shouldn't come home until five. So what? It was her house, too. She had every right to be there and was tired of feeling like she was a box of shirts, moved so easily from place to place.

———

Fitz's beat-up Ford Falcon was in front of the house. It was a soft butter yellow and had a bunch of dents, the silver metal showing through the paint.

Lucy stood on the front porch and stared at their door. Did she just barge in? Would barging in make Dad feel even more like she needed to go stay with Grandma and Grandpa? Was it possible to barge in to your own house?

Why did she need to worry all the time, anyway, and second-guess every single thought? And other people's thoughts? Why couldn't she just say the things that came into her head, like Gia?

Lucy pushed the front door open and stomped down the creaky hall into the living room, where Fitz sat in front of Dad on a stool, about to wrap gauze around Dad's stump, which Lucy had never seen before. The end of the stump was red and seemed swollen, the jagged scar puckered and angry-looking. Dad grimaced in pain, eyes closed.

"What's the matter?" Lucy said, before she could stop herself.

Dad's eyes flew open, probably thinking she was Mom come home from work. "Out of here, right now!"

"But—"

"Out!" Dad said, turning away from her and putting a protective hand over his stump.

Lucy, being stunned for the second time in one day, turned around and stiffly walked outside without a single word. She sat on the porch step and put her chin in her hands, too wrung out to cry. Numb. The way her arm felt when she'd slept on it wrong, only it was her whole body.

Then she began to tremble—a regular five, maybe, on the Richter scale.

Lucy wrapped her arms around her knees and rode out the trembles while she watched some kids kicking a ball around in the street. There was no rhyme or reason to their game. She tried to figure it out, to give her mind something to do, but if they were playing with rules, she had no idea what they were. She recognized Billy Shoemaker from around the corner, even though he'd buzz-cut his blond hair, and a few of his friends that lived in the other direction. Maybe seven in all. They looked like they were being simultaneously attacked by a swarm of gnats—ducking and swatting—and trying to kill each other with the ball. They tackled, kicked and chased each other with it.

It was positively baffling.

As Lucy's horrendous luck would have it, the ball came flying in her direction, rolling right up to her feet. A perfect opportunity for the boys to harass and tease her about her knock-knees and her tightly wound braids, just like they did all year. And if they did, she decided right then and there, she would walk into the house with their ball and pop it with a screwdriver from the junk drawer in the kitchen.

"Rossi!" Billy shouted, hand shading his eyes.

"What?"

"Come on! You any good at Crazy Kick Ball Tag? If you play, the teams will be even."

Lucy sat there, stunned for the third time, but stood up anyway. "What are the rules?"

"We make them up as we go along."

Lucy walked over to the group of boys who had teased her this year, holding the ball. She could feel the heat of the asphalt through the thin soles of her Keds.

"Evans, you switch. Lucy's on my team," Billy said.

The boys all whined, but did as they were told. "You just want her because she has a good arm," Evans said.

It was true. Lucy had always been one of the first kids

picked for teams during physical education class. The only time she was ever picked for anything, her arm being better than her temperament, apparently.

Billy Shoemaker waggled his eyebrows at her, which reminded Lucy of Milo, and thinking of Milo just made her angry all over again.

Lucy threw the ball at Billy, hard, in the stomach. "Did I win?"

"Ooof" was all he said. But he said it with a smile, while the other boys made all sorts of goofy sounds, "Aw, man!" and "Whoa," and "Don't mess with the Bossy Rossi!"

Crazy Kick Ball Tag was a vicious game. And there *were* gnats after all, hence the flailing around. The trick was remembering each of the made-up rules, which kept getting added as kids were tagged. You got knocked out if you couldn't recite all the rules in the right order.

Lucy embraced her newly discovered rage—and her confusion, and her frustration with the unfairness of the world—and took it out on every single one of those boys. She tossed and kicked the ball with perfect aim and fury. They took it easy on her at first—passing the ball gently, keeping their distance—because she was a girl, she supposed. But the first time Lucy decked Bernie Ryan with the ball to his chin, all bets were off. She scraped her knee and sweated through her braids and did the business of kicking each and every boy butt, teammates and opponents alike. It ended up Lucy against all seven of them.

Of course, Lucy was the last one standing.

After they all stood around for a while, catching their breath in the warm late-afternoon air and punching each other in the arm, reliving the best moments of the game, Billy said, "Mom's making a pizza. Wanna come for a slice?"

But Lucy was smack out of energy, and now shocked for the fourth time in one day. So enough was enough. "Maybe next time."

"Oh, there will be a next time," Bernie Ryan said with a smirk.

"See you later, Boss!" Billy called.

Boss. Lucy supposed she could live with that.

———

The boys went off in a pack; a couple even waved back at her. When she turned around to face the house, Fitz was sitting on the porch step, smoking a cigarette.

"If Mom catches you smoking around me, you'll be dead. She's a health nut," Lucy said as she sat down beside him.

"I'll take her over you any day. I thought that one boy was going to need my services when you were done with him," Fitz said.

Lucy was embarrassed. She'd lost her composure out there with those boys. "I wasn't *trying* to hurt him."

Fitz laughed. His teeth were just as big as he was, and very white. Lucy wondered if extra-white teeth were genetically linked to super-red hair. "I'd hate to see it if you were."

She picked up a dried leaf off the step. "Is there something extra wrong with Dad?"

"He needs to take better care of his stump," Fitz said. He blew the smoke away from her face.

"I read the manual you left from cover to cover," Lucy said, and quoted, "'The primary function of a prosthetic limb is to reestablish wholeness.'"

"Very good," Fitz said. "And what are you doing to reestablish wholeness?"

"What do you mean?" Lucy said. "I'm not missing anything."

"Hmmm," Fitz said, and put the cigarette out in the dirt.

He really was an extra-large person. Lucy wasn't sure how he fit into regular clothes, or his car for that matter. The color of his red-brown hair matched the color of the red-brown freckles splotched all over his pale skin. You'd never know, looking at that skin, that it was the middle of the summer.

"Why did he do that?" Lucy said, wanting to change the subject. "Hide his arm. That's not like him. This one time he slipped and fell in a pool of spilled water at the hospital and got a gash in his head. He needed nineteen stitches. He couldn't wait to show me."

"Everyone grieves differently," Fitz said.

"Grief? No one died."

"Grief is just a word for deep sorrow. We can feel deep sorrow for the loss of just about anything, right?"

"I was deeply sorrowful when I lost my favorite white sweater last year. That's not the same as when someone dies."

"No, it's not. But it doesn't mean you can't grieve the loss of that favorite white sweater."

Lucy considered that.

"Change is hard. Especially the kind of change your dad, you and your mom, your whole family, is going through. You probably had your life all planned out."

A strange car pulled into the end of the driveway just then. Mom was in the passenger seat. Lucy assumed the man driving was Mom's boss, Richard. She laughed at something Richard said. She didn't see them sitting there.

"Dad's alive, and that's all that matters," Lucy said, trying to talk herself into it.

Fitz didn't respond right away. He picked his cigarette butt out of the dirt and slid it into his pocket. "I tell my amputees that they used to be able to do ten thousand things, and now they can only do nine. That it's important to remember they can still do nine thousand things."

"Exactly," Lucy said. "You have to get back on the horse. Resilience is the most important thing."

"But I also tell them they need to grieve those one thousand things. Not forever. But for a time. And everyone's time is different. That is resilience, too."

Fitz was wrong. Thinking about the bad stuff was what made Lucy create a Homeostasis Extravaganza. It's what gave her the deep-down need to carry stones in her pockets every day.

Mom got out of the car with a smile on her face. She primped her hair, and when she noticed Lucy and Fitz on the steps, she frowned.

Fitz stood and reached a hand out to Lucy. She took it, and he helped her up. "I've seen lots of families. This one is going to be okay. Your dad is just throwing himself a little bit of a pity party at the moment. He'll get through it."

"Lucy! What are you doing here already?" Mom said.

Just then, Uncle G came screeching up in his truck and parked behind Mom. Gia sat in the passenger seat, leaning forward.

Uh-oh.

"I'm sorry!" Lucy said before Uncle G could start shouting.

But he didn't shout. He just kept stomping toward her, like a bear. Before Lucy knew what to think, or say, or what might happen to her in the next moment, Uncle G took her up into his big bear arms and hugged her so tight, she felt like a fried smelt, its guts loose and ready to slide right out.

"Don't you run off like that," he said. "We had no idea where you'd gone!"

"What did you do?" Dad said. Lucy looked up, and he stood just outside the front door.

Uncle G set her down. They were all staring at her, waiting for an answer.

Now was the time. She could tell them she was scared. That she didn't want to be sent away. She could admit all her worries about Dad, and Mom. She could tell them she'd be good from then on. Quiet. She'd be everyone's brave, strong girl.

Instead, she ran up the steps, past Dad, and left them all standing there frozen and silent.

a monsoon carp

*L*ucy couldn't stop thinking about Dad's arm. When she closed her eyes, she saw the misshapen and puckering red scar and wondered if it was supposed to look that way. But Dad didn't say anything about his arm, or getting mad at her. He just went to bed early that night, closing the door on her unasked questions.

Through the thin walls, her parents argued in angry half whispers. Mom angry with Dad for yelling at Lucy. Dad angry at Mom for getting a ride home from Richard. Dad not wanting Mom to work anymore. Mom finally yelling that she liked her job and wasn't going to be told what to do. Sometime later, long after Lucy should have been asleep, the front door slammed shut. The house became eerily still and quiet. So still and quiet, she could hear the loud ticking of the second hand on the clock above the stove around the corner.

Lucy needed to know which one of her parents had left,

even though she was sure she already knew, and so she tiptoed out of her room and stood in front of her parents' bedroom door. There was a wedge of light underneath that she'd grown used to over the months Dad had been gone. When she got up in the night to use the restroom or pour herself a glass of water, she saw the light under the door and knew her mom was still awake. Reading usually, but sometimes she'd hear her cry. Mom didn't like to cry in front of anyone, especially Lucy, because they were Chin-Up Women. They were Stiff-Upper-Lip Women. On those nights when Mom cried, Lucy would sit quietly outside the door, keeping Mom company, even if she didn't know it.

She didn't sit outside the door this time.

"Oh, Lucy. I'm sorry if we woke you," Mom said.

"I wasn't asleep."

Mom patted the bed beside her, and Lucy crawled in. Mom put her arms around Lucy and held her close. "Dad is having a hard time. We're all having a hard time."

"I don't know what to do," Lucy said.

"There's nothing for you to do."

But Lucy couldn't accept that. There had to be something. Something out there in the giant world, some therapy or medicine. Some combination of things that would help Dad through all this.

"Will he come back?" Lucy said.

"Oh, sweetheart. Of course he'll come back. You know how he walks to clear his mind. Why would you ask something like that?"

"No, I mean, will he come back to us? Will he ever be the way he used to be?"

"I have to believe he will."

Lucy wanted to tell Mom about the Mac and Cheese men. That she was worried there was something she might do, or even worse, something she should be doing that she wasn't, that might drive Dad away instead of drawing him close.

"Maybe you should quit your job," Lucy said. "What if he doesn't want to be married to someone who works?"

She looked up at her mom. Her beautiful, perfect mom, who even looked beautiful and perfect when she'd been crying and was wearing large pink curlers in her hair.

"Listen to me, Lucy. When people go through devastating events, they aren't themselves for a while. They get angry and afraid. They say and do things from that place of anger and fear. Try and remember it's the anger talking, not the person we love."

"What if he never stops being angry?"

Mom closed her eyes and set her curlered head against the headboard. "I don't know, Lucy. But I don't think that's going to happen."

"What if it does?"

She pulled Lucy closer. "I can't give you an answer that I don't have. But I can tell you I will fight for our family. I will fight with everything I have."

Lucy didn't doubt that was true, but it didn't make her feel much better.

The night after Lucy saw Dad's arm, she added an extra mist of Aqua Velva to her wrists. She opened her screenless window to the night and counted her stones out onto the windowsill, thinking about Milo, his reaction at the VFW, leaving her to fend for herself. How she was sure something was wrong, but had no idea what it might be or how to help.

It was still outside, windless, like the eye of a storm. Lucy had read all about storms last year, along with a thousand other subjects Ms. Lula had fed her. She thought about sixth grade, how alone she'd felt marching into the library at lunchtime. How she'd watched the Dandelion Girls from the window, and didn't get invited to a single birthday party.

And then, like a clap of thunder, she wondered, how could anyone have invited her anywhere if she spent every single day in the library? Alone? Ignoring everyone? It wasn't as though they'd driven her there with pitchforks. She'd gone there on her own. Every single day.

If Lucy was honest with herself, she hadn't given anyone at Millard McCollam Elementary much of a chance. She had lots of reasons for this. Good ones, even. Her dad was far away, and she was scared. She missed her Chicago friends and the families they'd known from Dad's residency. So Lucy had been prickly. Closed up like a clamshell. She had wanted to be alone.

Every single day.

What if she was the reason she didn't have any friends?

Lucy pored over her memories, looking for pieces of evidence that might support this theory.

They were everywhere.

Just before Linda McCollam had said, *Why can't you just be normal?* she'd said, *My cousin is in Vietnam, too.*

And what had Lucy said? *A cousin isn't the same as a father.*

How could she have said such a thing?

Because Linda McCollam was a Dandelion Girl? And Lucy wasn't?

Lucy didn't know.

There was more evidence. Billy Shoemaker teasing her. *Bossy Rossi! You ever gonna show us what you got, Bossy Rossi?* while he'd pitch to her during physical education, just like he teased everyone else.

Those boys today had said all manner of ridiculous and somewhat unhelpful things to each other, like they'd said to her last year.

Noodle arm!

Peter Perfect plaid pants!

Weenie bun! Weenie bun!

A bunch of shouts that didn't make any sense, pet names for each other, maybe. Things they understood because they had their own private language of friendship. The way she'd had with Rubin and Trina and Tabitha before she left Chicago. It didn't mean they were always insulting her. That was just their weird way of connecting.

And instead of taking it in the spirit it might have

been given, and maybe tossing a few of her own comments around, Lucy, instead, had taken it as one more reason to lock herself away in the library every day.

There was a knock on her door, and Dad stuck his head in. "I know you're too old for this, but can I tuck you in?"

Feeling too numb to be surprised, Lucy walked to the bed and settled in under her freshly laundered sheet. A comfort to her senses. She'd taken her braids out, and so she fanned her hair carefully on the pillow for the least amount of snarling.

Dad went to close the window. If he noticed her stones there, he didn't say anything.

"Leave it open," Lucy said. "I like to hear the night sounds."

"Those frogs sure are having a convention, aren't they? I wonder what they're talking about?"

"Frog politics. You know. Who's entitled to the best fly-catching spot, that sort of thing."

Dad smiled and sat on the bed beside Lucy. He brushed her hair back from her forehead.

"I'm so sorry, Lucy. You caught me off guard."

"It's okay. I shouldn't have come home anyway. I was early."

Dad didn't correct her. "Things won't always be like this."

Lucy didn't know if she could believe him. He didn't look her in the eye.

Dad picked up one of the black-and-white photos off her nightstand. "Any luck with your search?"

Lucy didn't want to change the subject. She wanted to

talk to her dad the way she always had, about her worries and fears. But she worried that might make her seem afraid, weak, maybe, and she wanted Dad to believe she was his brave, strong girl. Now more than ever.

"Tell me a story," Lucy said instead.

When Dad had been in medical school, she didn't get to see him much, and certainly not for bedtime stories. But on rare evenings, he'd be there, and he'd tell her a story from his childhood, or one about their huge and sprawling Italian family. Since she hadn't been able to spend much time with them, living so far away, she got to know her family one story at a time, until she moved out last year and those stories had come to life.

"Tell me your love story," Lucy said. Because it was her favorite of them all. The way Mom and Dad fell in love at first sight reminded her that anything was possible. And maybe that was all she needed just then.

"I've told you that story a thousand times," Dad said. "You probably know it better than I do."

Dad picked at a snag in the crocheted pillow Nonnina had made for Lucy years before she died. He didn't say anything more, which broke Lucy's heart just a little more than it was already broken.

She tried something different. "Can you tell me something about the war that wasn't horrible?"

Dad scratched at the stubble on his chin, pondering. He smiled. "Did I ever write to you about the monsoon and the carp?"

Lucy shook her head.

It was his first day in Vietnam, he explained, and there'd been a monsoon—no one knew the definition of *wet* until they'd been in a monsoon, he'd have her know—that had flooded the barracks he'd have to stay in until his officer's quarters were ready.

"The water rose, and the cots floated around like pool mattresses, and wouldn't you know, right there in the middle of the room was a carp the size of Rhode Island."

Lucy closed her eyes and imagined a giant carp swimming around her room, what she might do.

"We had half a platoon wanting to catch that fish and bring it down to the river, and the other half wanting to eat it. It was bedlam!"

Dad went on to tell her he had to stand on a floating cot to try and get their attention, to bring some sort of order, but he fell off sideways and splashed into two feet of water. When Dad stood up, spluttering, everyone was laughing so hard, they let him decide. And because it was a wily fish, it took them a while to catch him. They ended up using balled-up pieces of Wonder Bread.

"What did you do? Cook him or throw him back?" Lucy said. She'd sat up in bed, her hair a fluffy monster beast, but she didn't care.

"Well, after naming him Wonder Bread, of course, even the men who'd wanted to eat him had changed their minds. It's hard to eat something with a name. So, during one of the worst monsoons I would experience in the whole ten months I was there, we all marched down to the swollen river with Wonder Bread swimming around in a five-gallon bucket. One of the guys complained that now we'd have to eat spaghetti again! And so, we sang, all of us, 'On Top of Spaghetti' while we marched to set that fish free."

Lucy could see a big rowdy bunch of boys, just like the ones she'd been playing Crazy Kick Ball Tag with, only a little older, all singing at the tops of their lungs in the middle of a Vietnam monsoon, and the picture made so much unlikely sense that she laughed out loud, and Dad laughed right along with her.

For a moment, it seemed he'd come back to her. Just like he'd promised.

Then she ruined it.

"Did those boys all make it?"

Dad closed his eyes. Rubbed at his temples. "No, they didn't. I'm sorry to say, they didn't."

Those boys today. Twelve years old. Maybe thirteen. If there was still a war in another five years, which, who knew? The war had been going on since 1954, if you were to get right down to it. They'd all be doomed to a scene like the one Dad had just described, and maybe even die.

It was too much. Lucy pulled the sheet under her chin.

"Go to sleep, Lucia, my brave, strong girl."

Dad switched off the light and stood, forgetting her kiss good night. He closed the door behind him.

From a short distance, drifting through her open window, Lucy could hear Gia playing James Taylor. "Sweet

Baby James." The melody was like a lullaby and danced itself through the stillness of the night. Lucy crossed to the window and collected her stones. One by one, she laid them on her chest, feeling the weight of them through her nightgown. That weight was all that was holding her together.

even in the stars

*a*t first Lucy was as understanding as understanding could be about Milo not calling. By Saturday, though, she got mad. Milo wasn't the only one who'd suffered. Those jerks at the American Legion and the Veterans of Foreign Wars had insulted her, too. Her father gave his arm for his country, and those old men acted like World War II was the only proper way to lose an arm. Or die.

But she'd been busy helping finish up preparations for Dad's party, too. Lucy helped stuff cannoli and ravioli, sausages and pork butts, until her fingertips had turned to prune. It seemed to her that Italians were always stuffing one thing into another.

Alongside all that, Grandma and Grandpa Miller were coming. And Lucy was positive they would try and take her with them when they left.

Lucy could have used a friend.

On Saturday night, Grandma and Grandpa Miller arrived from Sacramento in a cloud of Shalimar and cigar smoke. Grandpa had wanted to drive down the day of the party itself, and then turn around and drive home, anxious as he was not to leave his television set and the *Wide World of Sports*, or whatever other sports they televised every weekend, for longer than he had to. Grandpa was convinced sports taught a person everything they needed to know about life, and apparently needed to be reminded every weekend. Qualities, he said, like grit and valor and teamwork. He was a World War II veteran, a naval aviator who had flown in the Pacific Theater. He never talked about it, but after her experience at the American Legion, Lucy was nervous for how Grandpa really felt about Dad and Vietnam. It had never occurred to her to ask.

But instead of coming down on Sunday, they came a day early because Grandma had insisted she could be of good use in helping prepare for the party. Neither Mom nor Lucy had the heart to tell Grandma she'd missed her opportunity. That they'd been preparing for a week and the only help she might give at the last minute was to offer up a refrigerator to store the bounty. So, unless they strapped an extra refrigerator to the top of their Lincoln Continental, with the leather seats and the automatic windows, there wasn't anything left to do.

As soon as they arrived, giving their usual pecks to the

cheek, like a bunch of birds, Grandpa Miller made a beeline for the Giants game on the television set—they'd scheduled their drive so he could make it in time for first pitch at Dodger Stadium—and propped himself on the sofa next to Dad with a whiskey on the rocks. He was thin, fidgety, and played golf most days, so that the skin on his arms, face and neck was tanned, in contrast to his full white mustache and head of hair. Grandpa had a tattoo of a hula dancer on his forearm that he could make dance by flexing his biceps. When Lucy was little, she'd asked who the young woman was, and Grandpa said it was Grandma. But Lucy had her doubts. So did Grandma.

Grandpa, his deep voice carrying across the room, asked Dad about Stanford Hospital and what his prospects were. Lucy tried hard to hear what Dad said, something about Stanford and the board of directors, but Grandma Miller's endless talking drowned him out.

As Mom and Lucy prepared dinner, Grandma leaned her bony hip against the kitchen cabinet and talked about how her new hairstyle required almost a whole can of aerosol to keep the fluff in place, how a good friend's daughter had just employed a maid and wasn't that something? And how her garden club was filled with ninnies who were turning old before their time. Grandma had long red nails that she flicked around for emphasis when she talked, which was slightly hypnotizing. They were not Press-On Nails.

Mom handed her a carrot. "Chop," she said.

Grandma looked at her nails. "Give me some bread. I can butter the bread."

"We're not having bread, Mom. We're having a salad."

"Who doesn't have bread with dinner?" Grandma went to the refrigerator and took out a loaf of bread that Dad used for his sandwiches. "This will do."

Grandma often ignored Mom's directions. Mom never argued. But Lucy noticed that the longer Grandma talked, the higher Mom's shoulders rose until they were almost in full-on shrug position.

"Oh! And I found this delightful little dress Lucy can wear to the party tomorrow," Grandma said, and vanished into the spare room. She came back out with a dress on a silk hanger. "Isn't it fabulous?"

And it was. It was pure white cotton with a smocked front and a little bit of lace edging. No sleeves. A proper summer sundress. Lucy ordinarily loved Grandma's dresses. She had spectacular taste and positively understood Lucy's sense of style. But Lucy had already meticulously chosen her outfit for the occasion, a ruffled blouse and a nice pair of shorts, so she could keep her rocks in the pockets for easy counting.

Lucy took hold of the dress, praising its beauty. She squeezed and searched. There were, in fact, no pockets.

Grandma narrowed her eyes. "Don't you patronize me. If you don't like it, just say so. I can't stand a puffer." A puffer was Grandma's term for a liar, basically. *A person who spewed more compliments than sense.* "What is it, grandchild? Speak up."

So Lucy did. "It doesn't have pockets."

Grandma blinked at Lucy. Then she blinked at Mom. Lucy was almost afraid to look at Mom, important as it was to her that they always make a good impression. On top of Mom's job and everything else going on, with Lucy's help, Mom had spent the last two days scrubbing every inch of their little house. Lucy could have eaten off the toilet bowl cover. Practically speaking, anyway.

Lucy forced herself to look at Mom, who was looking straight back, not with anger or mortification or disappointment, but with pride, it seemed. Her chin was lifted, and her shoulders had gone down to their regular position.

Grandpa walked into the kitchen from watching the game and took the whiskey down from the cabinet.

"Pockets? That must be a new style I am unaware of," Grandma sniffed.

"It's fine, Grandma. I love it. You always pick just the right dress. I don't have a white one."

The sad and sorry thing was, Lucy absolutely loved it and would have worn it to Dad's party in a flash. But the idea of not being able to count her stones made her stomach lurch up into her esophagus, nearly missing her epiglottis, or so it felt.

Lucy went to give Grandma the expected peck on her powdered cheek, even if Grandma was slightly prickly about it. The way she was prickly about most things.

"Oh, for heaven's sake, Loretta, you've got to be a better team player," Grandpa said. Then he winked at Lucy and walked out.

Grandma fluffed a napkin at his back just when the crowd on the television in the other room roared as Bobby Bonds knocked one out to right field, and Willie Mays slid into home base.

Just before midnight, Lucy woke to the sound of knocking against wood. She sat up in bed and saw Milo's round face through the open window, like a dark moon. Her room was filled with the sounds of midnight crickets and frogs.

"What are you doing?" Lucy whispered.

"I couldn't sleep."

"And how's that my problem?" Lucy crossed her arms.

They looked at each other.

"I shouldn't have left you the other day, okay? I just got so mad!" Milo said.

"I did, too. Did you ever think of that?"

"Sure I did. I only went a couple of blocks before I turned around, but you were already gone. Then I got lost. Then I was too embarrassed to call. There, now you have a map to all the feelings of Milo Cornwallace for the last three days. Happy?"

"Yes, actually. Thank you." Lucy uncrossed her arms.

"What are these?" Milo touched the stones on her windowsill, and Lucy had to fight to keep from yelling at him to Stop. Right. This. Second.

Instead, she scooped them up and put them under her pillow. "They're rocks, silly."

"Hmmm. Okay, well. I made a telescope. I wanted to try it out."

"Couldn't we have done this at a more decent hour? I have to get up early in the morning."

"It's more exciting in the middle of the night. Come on. The moon's going below the trees soon. Just for a few minutes."

Lucy threw on shorts under her knee-length nightgown and a sweatshirt, and climbed out the window, which was not as easy as it looked on television. She scraped her shin and tumbled into a heap on the patchy grass. Milo helped her up as she brushed the dirt from her behind, the leaf bits from her hair. He smelled like wood smoke.

"According to the *Farmer's Almanac*, we might be able to see the northern lights this week," Milo said.

"Really? The whole reason Nonnina wanted to take a cruise to Alaska was to see the aurora borealis. They'd been saving their tips for a long time before she died," Lucy said. "Did your grandma tell you she gave Papo his last dollar?"

"She did," Milo said. "When is he going?"

"I don't know."

Lucy wondered if he would go. If he might take Great-Aunt Lilliana with him for real-life company. Or if he'd just take Nonnina's urn.

There was a clearing near the creek where they could see a patch of sky through the trees, so Milo spread a towel over the dew-covered field sedge. Lucy sat down while he took a contraption out of his rucksack. The creek burbled in the background, and she suddenly felt nervous. Maybe she wasn't ready for the stars, tied as they were to the memory of how things were before Dad left for the war.

"I built it with stuff from Grams' attic."

He held the telescope out to Lucy like a prize. It was surprisingly heavy for something that was slightly bigger than a paper towel tube. It was rather clunky, and she had no confidence the homemade contraption would work. The same way she had no confidence in TV antennae, discounted bananas, or the fact that astronauts actually drank Tang in space.

Lucy lay flat on her back, eyes closed, the telescope lying against her chest.

"Go on, what are you waiting for?" Milo said.

With a deep and painful breath, Lucy placed the small end of the telescope against her eye socket, prepared for the sadness to hit her, the memory of Dad telling her he was leaving for Vietnam to come back in living color. Instead, the whole sky lit up through that little lens, magnifying the stars, more up close and personal than she'd ever seen before. Which, to her surprise, made her heart swell, instead of break.

"This is stupendous! How did you do it?"

"I built one last year after I wrote a book report. I remembered the instructions."

"Do you have a photographic memory?"

"No. Just a good one. For some things."

Lucy found the crooked handle of the Big Dipper in the sky and took a chance on herself and her feelings. "Dad used to take me to the roof of our apartment building in Chicago to look at the stars. But we didn't have a telescope," Lucy said. She told him the rest, about the Joes and Great-Aunt Lilliana's premonitions. That her father was the moon.

"Premonitions?"

"She thinks she can see the future. Sometimes she knows things, too. Secrets. But it's not that she's psychic. She's just smart and puts the clues together."

"She knew I wouldn't want to go to the cemetery," Milo said. "That was true."

Lucy rolled her eyes in the dark. "Lots of people don't like cemeteries. It was a good guess."

"Hmmmm."

Milo reached for the telescope, and Lucy let him take it. He peered up.

"Did you know it takes millions of years for the light of a star to reach our eyes? So, looking at the night sky is like looking back in time," Milo said. "It's like all the days of your life are up there, reminding you of what you've survived."

Lucy knew beauty. She'd seen it in the brushstrokes of paintings, and heard it in the lyrics of a song, or when a bow touched a violin string. But she'd never felt the beauty of an idea the way she did just then. Lucy had always seen Dad's leaving up there in the sky, but hadn't considered that everyone else's past was up there, too. This idea that she wasn't alone, even in the stars, shifted something inside, reminding her of the time their apartment had lost power during a snowstorm in Chicago and then, suddenly, in the middle of the second night, the lights flashed on, and everything was new.

Lucy also knew sadness. And could recognize it in someone else.

"Is there something wrong?" she asked. "Something besides your dad being in Vietnam?"

Milo didn't look away from the telescope. "I don't want to talk about it."

"Okay. But you can trust me, you know. I've never once told anyone's secret. My brain is a vault of interesting secrets."

"Like what?" Milo said. Then he looked at her and waggled both his eyebrows up and down, which she could see in the dim light.

"Very funny."

"Are you excited for your dad's party tomorrow?"

"More nervous than anything. I'm nervous about calamity, and I'm afraid my grandparents are going to try and take me back to Sacramento with them when they leave. Scratch that. I know they're going to try. I'm more afraid my mom will let them."

Milo suddenly sat up. "You can't let them do that."

"I won't."

"We have a job to do!" Milo's voice was high-pitched, slightly screamy.

"Don't worry. I don't think anyone will force me into a car. And short of that, I'll just refuse. Tie myself to a bedpost if I have to. Run away to your house and hide."

At first Lucy said this as a comfort to herself and Milo. But slowly she began to feel the truth of it. She would refuse, and this knowledge filled her with confidence.

For a while, they passed the telescope back and forth, but no aurora borealis.

"The almanac said we should be able to see it. But I think we're too far south," Milo said.

"Too many trees," Lucy said.

"It was worth a try."

When Lucy handed Milo the telescope for the last time, his fingers brushed the back of her hand. They were warm even though the night was cool.

"We can go see my school librarian next week. I bet she can help us track down clues. She works down at the city library during the summer."

"I went to visit Doreen yesterday. Mac and Cheese had gone up into the attic and found three boxes of sign-in books that go back to 1960. That's when they opened their doors."

"I don't know if I want to go back there. I can't believe Mac sent us to the American Legion and the VFW."

"They just didn't figure they'd be that awful to a couple of kids. Mac's sorry. He feels terrible."

Lucy wasn't sure it mattered that they were sorry. How was she supposed to trust them now?

"They wanted us to come over and look through the books with them," Milo said. "A lot of the men who come to the meetings want to help out, too. Mac said we started something important. He said some of the men who come to the meetings and never talk about the war are talking about the war."

Lucy thought about that. How one small thing could be connected to something else and something else after that, a long string of connected things that ended up spreading wider and wider until maybe that one small thing ended up being connected to everything. Sort of like her family.

And maybe even Lucy.

She supposed this was the serendipity Uncle G was talking about.

Farther down the creek, the crickets and frogs had taken up where they'd left off before Lucy and Milo had come crashing into their world. A cloud passed over the three-quarter moon, and Lucy didn't want to move. She just wanted to lie there in the dim moonlight listening to the sounds of Uncle G's woods and pretend there was no tomorrow. That none of her relatives would embarrass her in front of Milo. Again. That the party would go off without a hitch.

"Where do the dragonflies sleep?" Lucy suddenly wondered.

"Everywhere," Milo said.

Everywhere. Lucy liked that idea. Like wherever she was, at least in the summertime, day or night, there was probably a dragonfly close by. For all the summers to come, Lucy knew, she would remember this fact and think of Milo.

"You can't let your grandparents take you," Milo said. Unexpectedly, he took Lucy's hand and held tight as they looked up at the stars.

Then, feeling the warmth of his hand in hers, she realized she wanted more than to *have* a friend.

She wanted to *be* a friend.

into the wolf's mouth

*L*ucy woke with a rather large pit in her stomach in antici-pation of the day. And not the fruit kind, either. The kind of pit that seemed it might swallow her instead of the other way around.

The house was quiet, and so she tiptoed to the kitchen for a glass of orange juice before anyone was up, hoping for a moment of peace and quiet. Orange juice, with its sweet-tart shock to the taste buds, had a way of cheering her and preparing her for the day.

"You're up early, grandchild," a voice called from the living room.

Grandma Miller. She sat on the old brown sofa, her hair already perfectly coiffed, false eyelashes applied, something white balled in her lap. Lucy feared it was the dress, had no idea what Grandma might be doing to it. She was funny about holding little grudges, like the time

Grandma had asked Lucy if she liked the color mustard, to which Lucy had replied that no, she did not like the color mustard, only to find out Grandma had painted her house a bright, flaming mustard that reminded Lucy of Linda McCollam's argyle socks. Grandma was snippy about it for the next two phone calls.

"Would you like some orange juice, Grandma?"

"That would be delightful."

Lucy poured them each a glass and walked into the living room. She took two plastic coasters off the table next to Dad's BarcaLounger and set them side by side on the coffee table. Then she sat down dutifully next to her grandma and prepared for the worst.

"There," Grandma said, and held up the white dress.

"What?"

"I used an old sheet your mom had and sewed you some pockets."

Of all the shocks Lucy had received in the last few days, this was the biggest, most outrageous shock of them all.

"A thank-you would be nice," Grandma said.

"Oh, Grandma! Thank you!" Lucy said, and threw herself into Grandma's arms, which was entirely unlike her *and* Grandma.

"Go on, start getting yourself ready. You certainly can't go with your hair like that."

"But we don't have to be there for six hours."

"You can never start the beautification process too soon," Grandma said.

Lucy patted her hair. It was quite voluminous. She rushed into her room to tightly braid it into place.

It didn't take long for everyone else to rise and shine and drink orange juice and get ready for the day. Mom, Grandma and Lucy played gin rummy most of the morning while Grandma talked and talked.

Grandpa, of course, watched the *Wide World of Sports* until it was time to leave, but not before he'd seen Lucy's copy of Milo's drawing with the symbol of the Dirty Thirty and the pictures of the family on her nightstand table. He'd come in to see if she wanted to ride with them in the Lincoln Continental.

"Whatcha got there, sport?"

Lucy nervously explained their quest. How Milo wanted to find the family so they could have their Purple Heart. She tried to read Grandpa's face, his blue, blue eyes, to see if he thought that was a dumb idea or, worse, if he might feel the same as those men at the American Legion.

"He's quite an artist, your Milo," Grandpa said, studying the drawing.

Finally, Lucy couldn't take it anymore. "Grandpa, I need to know if you think Vietnam veterans are bums."

"What?"

"Some people think Vietnam veterans don't deserve the same amount of respect as other veterans because they think they're all on drugs or something. Or that they're doing terrible things over there to innocent people."

"Where did you get that idea?"

Lucy concentrated on the comb lines in Grandpa's fine white hair. "We went to the American Legion and the VFW for some help. There was a guy who got angry and said it was a dirty war and a bunch of other stuff about Vietnam veterans."

Grandpa's face turned pink, then red. "You listen to me. Those boys over there have nothing to do with politics. They're doing what they're told. And they're putting their lives on the line, just like I did. No different."

He took a white handkerchief out of his back pocket and dabbed his forehead. Lucy knew Grandma ironed those white handkerchiefs, had seen the tiny perfect stack of them in Grandpa's dresser drawer.

He stood tall, even though he wasn't. "Your dad is a hero. And don't you let anyone tell you different." Then he took Lucy into his arms. "Don't let anyone tell you different."

"I won't, Grandpa."

After the eventful morning and early afternoon, Grandma and Grandpa Miller finally left for Papo Angelo's in the Lincoln. Dad, after closing himself up in their bedroom for twenty minutes, came out wearing his prosthetic arm under a long-sleeved cotton shirt that he'd rolled up to the elbows. The prosthetic stuck out at a stiff angle in front of him, like he was waiting for a falcon to land, and Lucy could see the lumps under his shirt from all the bands and buckles that kept it strapped firmly in place. The only time Lucy had felt more relieved was when Dad stepped off the plane and she saw with her own two eyes that he was alive.

Instead of a hand at the end of the prosthetic, there was

a metal hook with a clamp that was probably meant to help Dad grasp. "I think it will be easier to get through the party with a fake arm than a missing one. Easier to pretend nothing is amiss."

Lucy could see how that was logical, but couldn't help but feel ignored. That her family's feelings were more important to Dad than hers.

"I don't know if I'm more a spectacle with it or without it," Dad said.

"You were born a spectacle," Mom said. She smiled at Dad. He smiled back, big and wide, and Lucy thought, if only for a moment, everything was how it used to be.

———————

Papo Angelo's house was directly next door to the San Jose Fire Department, Station 16, Battalion 2. Often, his Sunday night dinners would be accompanied by sirens and flashing red lights coming through the dining room window. When that happened, Papo Angelo would raise his glass and shout, "*In bocca al lupo!*" and the family would shout back, "*Crepi!*"

Which meant "Into the wolf's mouth!" and "May he choke and die!"

Or, basically, break a leg.

So it was no surprise to Lucy that the firemen stood around with everyone else on the lawn and in the driveway waiting for them to get there. She noticed Milo and Mrs.

Bartolo standing amongst the aunts and Hairy Uncles, the cousins and second cousins and all the family friends. So many people, in fact, that when she was younger, Dad had made her a chart to keep them all straight.

"*Salute!*" all the lawn people roared as soon as Dad got out of the car. He went to raise the stiff prosthetic, realized he couldn't because of all the straps and buckles, and raised the other hand instead. Great-Uncle Lando shoved a glass of pink champagne in it, and then they all mobbed him.

In a panic, Lucy flung herself out the car door and tried to make her way through the crowd to get to Dad, to make sure he wasn't going to have another shaking attack like he'd had at the airport, but when she got close enough, she saw he was laughing and hugging, patting backs and kissing cheeks. Mom gave him enough space to let his family love all over him, so Lucy took herself and her racing heart straight to where Milo stood.

"Hi, Mrs. Bartolo. Thanks for coming," Lucy said.

Mrs. Bartolo wore a Happy New Year tiara and blew a horn in her face. "I never miss a party!" she said.

Milo had changed his uniform. Today he wore a nice pair of pressed khaki pants and a blue collared shirt that he kept fidgeting with. He still wore his Converse, though, and his glasses glinted in the sunlight. His blond bristly hair reminded her of a horsehair brush.

"This is something else," Milo said. He held up a plastic champagne glass filled with what Lucy knew was sparkling apple cider. Great-Uncle Lando was known to walk around with a bottle of both apple cider and pink champagne, filling and refilling glasses.

Lucy took it from him and swigged the whole thing down, then wiped her mouth. "Let's go see if we can help Great-Aunt Lilliana. It's always worse if she has to come looking for you."

"Your dress is beautiful," a voice said from behind her.

Lucy turned around. It was Gia, with Josh right beside her. And whether Lucy wanted her to or not, Gia gave Lucy a tight squeeze. "I'm sorry you missed Papo's last dollar. I wish you could have been there."

"It's okay," Lucy said. "I'm sorry I screamed at you."

Lucy wanted to stop being mad at her cousin. Not just about Papo's dollar, but the fact that Gia had gotten older and left Lucy behind. Maybe that's what Lucy had mostly been mad about all along. It was like a knot in her hair, all that anger. Hard to untangle.

Josh pulled on Lucy's right braid, just like always. Then Gia and Josh were pushed along in the crowd.

Lucy wanted to introduce Milo to Mom and Dad, but figured now wasn't the time. The large crowd of lawn people moved to the side of the house and through the gate into the large, grassy backyard, where someone, Uncle Joe Senior most likely, was playing the accordion music Dad loved so much. Lucy and Milo squeezed through the crowd, and after Milo found Mrs. Bartolo a nice place to sit in the shade of Nonnina's fig tree, right next to a rip-roaring game of bocce ball, they both headed for the back door and the kitchen just inside.

"Lucy!"

Grandma Miller. How could she forget about Grandma Miller?

She and Grandpa were standing a bit stiffly by the table of antipasto salads that had been set out before lunch was served. It wasn't that they didn't like Italian food, necessarily. It was that Grandpa was more of a "meat and potatoes sort of person," and all the sauces gave Grandma "indigestion." More than once, when Grandma and Grandpa had shown up for a Rossi family event, Grandma had snuck food out of her purse. They were fans of hot dogs, salads without dressing, and pot roast with mushy carrots. Lucy had given up on their taste buds long ago.

"And who might this be?" Grandpa said, looking Milo up and down.

"This is Milo. He's the one I told you about. He's here for the summer, staying with his grandma."

"Nice to meet you, sir," Milo said, and shook Grandpa's hand.

"Now, that's how we should raise our American youth!" Grandpa said, and clapped him on the back.

"Can you be a dear and find me some of that grape soda?" Grandma said. She fanned herself with a paper doily that she'd taken from under the small plate of *affettati misti*. "You know how much I love your papo's secret stash."

"Sure thing, Grandma."

Lucy and Milo zoomed into the kitchen. Nonnina's pink kitchen where the cabinets were pink, the tile counters were pink. Even the refrigerator and stove were Pepto-Bismol pink. Which was enough to make any person in their right mind stop and look around in wonder.

"Holy moly!" Milo said. "It's even more pink than the deli!"

Great-Aunt Lilliana stood on a short kitchen stool and stirred the polenta in a saucepot big enough to hold one of the Joes. A slightly less gigantic saucepot simmered with the *sugo* meat, or sauce-soaked meat, and marinara Lucy could smell bubbling away in its cauldron.

Lucy dug through Papo's fridge—past the cranberry juice Papo drank for a healthy bladder, and the dandelion wine—and found the grape soda all the way in the back. What Grandma didn't know was that Papo kept his special stash just for her.

"Stir the polenta, Lucy!" Great-Aunt Lilliana shouted like thunder from the sky. "And you, Milo, stir the sauce."

"But I—" Lucy started.

Milo immediately jumped to where Great-Aunt Lilliana was pointing and stirred the sauce. He waggled his eyebrows at Lucy.

"*Basta!*" Great-Aunt Lilliana tossed her hand in the air in Lucy's general direction, like she was tossing one of Uncle Joe's pizzas, and went to knead a hippopotamus-sized lump of dough. The rest of the aunts each had a task and moved around the kitchen in a frenzy.

Lucy looked for someone to deliver the drink to her grandma, but the only people nearby were two distant cousins from Fresno carrying their mother like the Queen of Sheba, on a throne of tattooed arms, from her spot in the living room to a spot at one of the outside tables. She laughed like a little girl.

Milo tried to hide a snickery smile as he watched the tattooed cousins, his chin tucked into his neck. He snorted, so Lucy snorted, and then Great-Aunt Lilliana shouted at them both, "Germs!"

"Is she calling us germs or afraid of them?" Milo whispered.

"I'll be right back, Great-Aunt Lilliana! I have to take a soda to Grandma Miller," Lucy said. Great-Aunt Lilliana threw her hand up in the air again and got Milo to stir the polenta, which would turn into a giant mass of glue if he didn't.

Just then, two of the Joes ran in, beelining for the stove. One of them grabbed a meatball out of the saucepot with his bare hands, just like a nincompoop. He yelped and tossed it to the other Joe. Back and forth they went, with Great-Aunt Lilliana shouting even more curse words, shooing them out with the rolling pin she always kept handy when the Joes were around.

Lucy hurriedly grabbed the glass of grape soda, turned around and promptly slipped in the tomato sauce spilled during the Joes' meatball-juggling act. In slow motion, it seemed to Lucy, the grape soda went flying all over her as she landed in the tomato sauce.

Lucy froze. The whole world froze. The Milky Way and the galaxies and all of time froze.

Then, as if that weren't bad enough, the sirens went off at the fire station next door.

"*In bocca al lupo!*" Papo Angelo shouted from outside, and it sounded like the whole world shouted back, "*Crepi!*"

"*Marone,*" Great-Aunt Lilliana said, looking Lucy up and down.

And wasn't that the truth.

al fine!

"Polenta waits for no one!" Great-Aunt Lilliana shouted and then blew a whistle, which brought aunts and cousins running. She directed one after the other to carry the pots of sauces and meats out to the tables while Lucy stood there covered in goop. Her pure white dress with pockets ruined.

Milo's mouth was a perfect O, but Great-Aunt Lilliana didn't let him come to Lucy's rescue. She sent him out with a fresh glass of grape soda for Grandma Miller, while she took Lucy by the arm and directed her to the spare bedroom. There, she slid open the closet door to all Nonnina's dresses that Papo never had the heart to get rid of. Great-Aunt Lilliana swept the hangers, her rings flashing, along the wooden post, until she came to a particular dress. It was orange eyelet with a cinched waist and buttons up the front. Lucy, not thinking much about her own modesty, just shrugged out of her white sundress and stood like a stick bug in her undershirt and underwear. Obediently, she put her hands up while Great-Aunt Lilliana slid the new dress over her head. It hung loose on her nonexistent hips, about two sizes too big. Great-Aunt Lilliana put on her rhinestone eyeglasses and inspected her from hair to toes.

"Here, I've got just the thing." Great-Aunt Lilliana crossed the room to a bleached-wood dresser and opened the top drawer. She pulled out a long silky scarf with sunflowers and wrapped it around and around Lucy's waist. "Some sunglasses, and you look like a young Audrey Hepburn."

Lucy peered in the floor-length mirror and was surprised to find it was true. She did have her dad's wide brown eyes. And Audrey Hepburn's nose wasn't all that tiny, either. Plus, the dress was pretty great, even if it was from the fifties.

"Let me just set this in some cold water," Great-Aunt Lilliana said, and picked the white dress up off the floor.

"No, I can do it," Lucy said, but it was too late. Great-Aunt Lilliana had discovered the rocks in her pockets.

"Is this something I should worry about?" Great-Aunt Lilliana said. She held out a handful of stones.

"Counting them calms me down," Lucy said with a shrug.

Great-Aunt Lilliana nodded and peered into Lucy's eyes. "Maybe you are Fattucchiera as well."

If she was Fattucchiera, it meant she'd know things deep in her Rossi bones. Lucy suddenly wondered how she ever could have thought superstition was such an unreasonable thing. In fact, wasn't her Homeostasis Extravaganza really just a fancy name for her superstitions?

Great-Aunt Lilliana rummaged around in Nonnina's closet and came back with a small purse, one with a long strap that could go across Lucy's body and over one shoulder. She helped Lucy transfer the stones, and then placed it over her head. She tucked in a sprig of rue for good luck, and Lucy didn't mind as much as she once might have.

"There. Now you are ready for whatever happens."

"I don't feel ready." Lucy was feeling like a sack of broken crackers again. Like she had when she'd first seen the Mac and Cheese men.

"Anyone can do anything a few hours at a time."

Lucy wondered if it could, in fact, be that easy. As easy as changing her mind.

It was.

———

Lucy and Great-Aunt Lilliana had been gone only ten minutes or so, and rushed out to help with the last of the food preparations. Four extra-long rectangular tables festooned with herbs and flowers and small American flags sat in a square around the courtyard. There was a water fountain in the corner, three frolicking angels with water spouting from their mouths and fingertips, one on each tier.

Papo sat in the center of one of the long tables, Nonnina's urn in the chair to his right, Dad sitting to his left. Each table had large planks of polished wood set on top, evenly spaced, instead of plates. Milo had saved Lucy a seat and so she scooted in next to him. Great-Uncle Lando sat on the other side of Milo, pouring him a glass of pink champagne instead of apple cider because Great-Uncle Lando had had enough champagne for himself by now and didn't know the difference anymore.

A couple of burly muscled family friends, Carlo and Chooch, walked out into the courtyard, each carrying the handle of the copper pot of polenta. Great-Aunt Lilliana stood in the center of the tables and directed the boys to set the pot down on a rolling cart. She held a large serving spoon up the way the Statue of Liberty holds her torch.

"*Al fine!*" Great-Aunt Lilliana said.

"*Al fine!*" the whole world responded.

Which meant "to the end."

To the end of what? Lucy wondered. The end of life? The end of time? The end of how much a person could take?

Great-Aunt Lilliana ceremoniously glopped the polenta out onto each of the plywood planks on each of the four tables, quickly designing the boot of Italy with her spoon. The Belly Button Aunts then followed with glops of sauce on top of the polenta.

"What is she doing?" Milo said, fork in hand.

"It's a family tradition. The wood is treated, like a cutting board. And we all eat together without the boundaries of a plate."

Lucy looked around for Grandma and Grandpa Miller

to see how they might be taking the news about eating off a plywood board instead of plates. She wasn't sure if Mom had warned them about the polenta, as she usually did about whatever they were having for dinner at Papo's house. They both sat next to Mom with matching looks of stunned incomprehension.

Lucy picked up her napkin to hide her unexpected fit of giggles.

"What?" Milo said, smiling along with her. Mrs. Bartolo sat on the other side of Great-Uncle Lando, who was explaining how pink champagne was manufactured by adding red wine to the white wine or by simply using grape skins, and wasn't that fascinating? Mrs. Bartolo giggled instead of saying that it was fascinating, which made Lucy laugh even more.

"Look at my grandparents," Lucy whispered. Grandma had her large black handbag in her lap and was digging around in it.

"Did your grandma just give your grandpa a sandwich?"

Lucy had to bend over into her napkin to keep herself from howling, and Milo laughed alongside her.

Finally, they turned to the board of polenta, and Lucy explained, "You take the meat and some sauce and just drop it over your portion of the polenta. See, my section is Calabria. You can have the boot. And don't stuff yourself. This is just the first course."

Milo didn't talk. He just ate. Lucy looked around at her family and watched Gia and Josh at the long table directly across from her, the Belly Button Aunts like bookends on either side. Gia was staring into her lap, and Josh had his long arm wrapped around her shoulder. He kissed her temple and whispered something into her ear. Gia nodded but didn't look up, and Lucy felt a shiver of longing. Not for the kiss, necessarily. The idea of someone's mouth on her face sounded about as tempting as being attacked by a swarm of bees. But Lucy knew Gia could tell Josh anything because she'd seen evidence of this over and over again. They'd lie in the backyard grass on a blanket whispering to each other and weaving daisies into each other's hair. She'd seen the way they looked at each other sometimes, like there was no one else in the universe but the two of them. They were connected by that invisible string she'd imagined, just like the rest of her family.

It wasn't fair.

After fifteen minutes or so, when everyone had taken the edge off their hunger, Papo Angelo stood and raised his glass. "I want to give a toast to my son. We're so grateful to have our boy home." He opened his mouth to go on, but instead broke down into tears, which made Lucy's throat grow tight. Dad stood up, and they hugged, clapping each other on the back.

What followed was a series of toasts to Dad.

Salute!

Cent'anni!

Cento di questi giorni!

Without even knowing it was happening until it was

happening, Lucy found herself standing with her own glass of sparkling apple cider in her hand, wanting desperately to feel that invisible string of connection.

"To my brave dad. I'm glad you're home."

The feelings of sadness and fear and anguish and longing came swooping in and took her breath away. Afraid of sobbing right there in the middle of her entire family, she sat down quickly and put on the bravest face she could find so Dad would know she was his brave, strong girl.

Dad stood up, walked all the way around the table and wrapped her with his good arm, taking her off her feet and swinging her around.

"My brave, strong girl," he whispered before setting her back on her feet.

There weren't any dry eyes left after that. Once Dad made it to his seat, after being thumped on the back and touched on the arm and attacked by the Joes, the volume of the conversation slowly turned up once again.

Soon, the plywood boards were removed and more food was put down in their place. Platters of rosemary-and-garlic-stuffed porchetta, herb-roasted potatoes, rotisserie chickens, plates of spicy Italian sausage, roasted red peppers and Great-Aunt Lilliana's famous dinner rolls. There were all sorts of sautéed vegetables that had come from many gardens, broccoli, asparagus and chard. Even Grandma and Grandpa Miller filled their plates with a few bites of the less spicy offerings.

Lucy looked around at her family, soaked them all in like

a roll in sauce and, for the first time, felt the tiniest thread of a connection. Because she loved them. Whatever their eccentricities, she loved them with every bit of her heart.

———————

It wouldn't be a Rossi family party without the dancing. Of course, Lucy would rather have turned her eyelids inside out than dance in her rather uncoordinated fashion in front of Milo, but the choice was out of her hands. "North to Alaska" came over the speakers, and Josh waved at her from where he was sitting with Gia.

"Come dance with me!" he shouted, and stood up to fetch her.

Lucy could not help but be fetched by Josh. She turned to Milo and shrugged, as if to say, *What are you going to do?*

Soon enough, everyone was dancing. Great-Uncle Lando was cheek to cheek with Great-Aunt Maria, even though it was a fast song, and the Joes chased each other in between the dancers. Lucy looked around for Mom and Dad, thinking it would be good to see them close together, reminding her of the times she'd caught them dancing in the living room or on the rooftop beside the barbecue grill in Chicago.

She didn't see them anywhere.

After bobbing up and down and calling it dancing, Lucy was relieved when the song finally ended and "Love Me Tender" came on, thinking Josh would go pull Gia onto the dance floor. But he didn't. He held his arms out to Lucy, and when she stepped forward, he took her hand and put it on his waist and took her other hand in his. There was about a foot of space between them as they rocked from one foot to the other. It was her first slow dance. And it happened to be with the boy she was sure she would love for the rest of her life.

"I wanted to talk to you," Josh said.

Lucy looked up into his hazel eyes and felt as though her bones had liquefied, making her quivery. She was angry at her bones for deserting her at such a time.

"You know the draft lottery is coming, right?" Josh said.

"August fifth."

"And you know I'm eligible for the draft."

All Lucy could do was nod.

"Gia's smart. She's brilliant. She'll end up going to Berkeley or Columbia or some other super-smart school. As smart as she is, she doesn't have a lot of common sense sometimes. Do you know what I mean by that?"

Lucy, unfortunately, knew exactly what Josh meant.

"She's passionate, and I swear she'd run into a burning building to save the animals or for women's rights or the hundreds of other causes she cares about. She'd run into a burning building for her family, for you," Josh said.

Even though all they ever managed to do was get on each other's nerves lately, Lucy knew that Gia loved her fiercely. The way she did everything fiercely.

"If I go to Vietnam, you'll know what she's going through," Josh said.

"Don't say that!" Lucy stopped her foot-to-foot swaying. "You're not going anywhere."

"I have a one-in-three chance of being drafted. I just want you to promise me that, even though Gia can be a pain in the butt, you'll help her. You know what's coming."

Lucy felt so many different things. Boneless from dancing with Josh. Terrified he'd go to Vietnam. Flattered he believed she was someone Gia needed.

Strong and capable, because she knew he was right.

The song ended, and Josh gave her a twirl, then hugged her close.

He smelled like Aqua Velva.

———————

When the party was over and most of the family had gone home, Lucy and Milo helped Great-Aunt Lilliana put the leftovers away in plastic containers to stock up Papo's fridge.

"What happened to the dress?"

It was Grandma Miller, of course, her voice shrill, even though Lucy had seen Great-Uncle Lando pouring lots of pink champagne into her glass.

"Grape soda explosion," Milo said. "And then she landed in some tomato sauce. It was gnarly," he finished.

"Great-Aunt Lilliana is soaking it in the bathtub," Lucy said. "I'm sorry, Grandma. But I don't think the stains are going to come out."

"Bring me a bucket, some white vinegar and baking

soda! Pronto!" Grandma dug under the kitchen sink and came out with a pair of rubber gloves.

"What's this?" Great-Aunt Lilliana came into the kitchen carrying a platter of chicken, Gia following close behind. "You're going to help with the cleaning, Loretta? Nonsense. Go sit down and enjoy some anisette."

Grandma held up her gloved hands like she was about to operate. "I'm going to save Lucy's dress!"

"Save her . . . Oh, I'm afraid it's too late for that," Great-Aunt Lilliana said. Then to Lucy, "Didn't Gia tell you?"

"Tell me what?" Lucy said, panicked. She rushed into the bathroom where she had left her dress, and found it tie-dyed an orange-red, like a sunset, and hanging from a line in the shower.

Lucy was completely speechless.

"It was ruined," Gia said. "There was no getting out the pasta sauce, so I ran home to see what was left of the dye I just used to tie-dye some shirts for me and Josh last week. I thought it would be a nice surprise."

"Well, I'll be," Grandma said. "That is some ingenuity at work."

Grandma didn't think much of tie-dye and hippies, but she was a sucker for ingenuity and people who used their brains.

Lucy touched the skirt. Somehow, Gia had made a bunch of small white circles into the shape of a heart on the chest. Great-Aunt Lilliana, Grandma, Milo and Gia all stood too close to each other in the small bathroom, fidgeting, staring at Lucy for a response, maybe.

"Can I have a minute?" Lucy said as calmly as she could.

"Of course!" Great-Aunt Lilliana said, and shooed them out. "Except Milo."

Milo turned back and closed the door. Lucy slid down the tile wall until she was sitting on the floor.

"That's quite a trick," Milo said. He tried to do the same thing, but his legs were too long and so his knees ended up close to his ears. They were quiet for a few minutes, watching the dress drip, drip, drip into the shower drain.

"It's just a dress," Milo said.

"Actually, I love it. I don't want to love it, but I do."

"Why don't you want to love it?"

"Because I still might be mad at Gia. I'm not ready for her to be nice to me, maybe."

"You can't love a dress and be mad at Gia at the same time? That is very complicated."

"Life is very complicated."

"Sure it is."

Milo stood up and snooped around the bathroom, which was also very pink. Just not as pink as the kitchen. He picked up the soap and smelled it.

"Why are you so mad at her, anyway?"

"I overheard some plans she had to protest at Travis Air Force Base. I've seen what those protests look like. They throw stuff at soldiers, and I don't think that's right. But it feels like a dumb reason to still be mad at her."

"This war makes people do crazy things."

"She just wants it all to end, I guess. Just like me," Lucy said. "Just like everyone."

Milo opened the medicine cabinet and took out a floral shower cap. Whether it had belonged to Nonnina or Great-Aunt Lilliana, Lucy wasn't sure.

"How do I look?" he said, putting it on.

"It lacks the element of surprise. I've already seen you in a shower cap. Although the flowers are nice."

Milo sat down on Great-Aunt Lilliana's makeup bench. He clicked on the lights around her makeup mirror and picked up a bright red lipstick.

"It's just a dress," he said again, and put on the lipstick. "And it's time to stop being mad at Gia."

Lucy laughed against her will at Milo's red lips. Then Milo laughed. Then he stopped laughing when, even after wiping away the lipstick, it had stained his lips a bright orange.

Which matched Lucy's new dress.

american legion, part two

On Tuesday, when Grandma and Grandpa Miller were set to go back home, Lucy woke up to Grandma's and Mom's harsh whispers coming from the kitchen.

"She needs a break from all . . . this," Grandma said. "You're working. Anthony is trying to heal and figure out what's coming next. The poor girl needs to relax."

Mom's voice: "I just don't feel like that's the right thing to do. Lucy would be devastated to be sent away, she's made a friend—"

"Who? That boy? He's only here for the summer, anyway. I could bring her back with me and introduce her to girls her own age. I've already talked to Lindy and Martha Ann. They both have girls going into junior high school. Same as Lucy. That boy is turning her wild."

"No one is turning anyone wild, Mom. They're kids."

"You told me what they've been doing. Digging up things that are better left buried. Visiting veterans' homes, places where the failures go. The ones who can't hack life anymore. The ones who've given up. What sort of environment is that for a girl?"

Lucy got herself dressed as quickly as she could and marched out into the kitchen. If they were going to decide her fate, she wanted them to do it with her standing right there in front of them.

Mom and Grandma stopped talking midsentence when she showed up.

"I don't want to go. I can't leave Milo, or Dad," Lucy said, feeling brave.

"See?" Grandma said. "She feels responsible."

Grandma already had a full face of makeup on, even though it was only eight in the morning. She looked like she was going to a cocktail party. Even her dress was perfectly pressed as though it hadn't come out of a suitcase. Lucy wondered how much time it took to make herself look just so. If Just So was worth it.

Dad and Grandpa sat outside at the patio table, reading sections of the *San Jose Mercury News*, sipping cups of coffee. A transistor radio sat between them on the table and Lucy could hear the news through the closed patio door.

Onetwothreefourfive-sixseveneightnineten.

Lucy looked at Mom, worried. Because Mom resembled a frayed shoestring. One quick tug, and she'd break in two. She didn't know if Mom could stand up to Grandma Miller and the fierceness with which she knew everything.

But Lucy knew something, too. She was not getting into

that Lincoln Continental with Grandma and Grandpa. Even if it did have real leather seats, air-conditioning and automatic windows.

———————

Before Grandma and Grandpa left, with the question of whether or not Lucy was going with them still looming, Grandpa insisted on taking Lucy for a ride.

"Twenty minutes, tops," Grandpa said. "There's something we have to do."

"Is this a trick? Because it won't work. I'm not going," Lucy said.

"It's not a trick. Come on."

The morning was cool, and Grandpa put on a light Windbreaker. He held the front door open for Lucy and she decided to trust him. She could imagine Grandma trying to trick her, but never Grandpa.

The inside of the car smelled warm and leathery, and Grandpa had the radio turned to an oldies-but-goodies station that played music from the fifties. There was lots of crooning and horn playing, and Lucy supposed she didn't mind all that much as they drove down the hill.

"I'm proud of you for standing up for yourself. That is an important skill," Grandpa said. He smoothed back his white hair with one hand. It was a little curly around the edges. "Grandma's not very happy about it. But that's just Grandma."

"Kids aren't supposed to stand up for themselves. It's disrespectful."

"Now you sound like your grandmother. There's a time and a place for most things. The trick is knowing which is which. And you, my dear granddaughter, know which is which."

The trees gave way to cement sidewalks, and Grandpa drove straight for Jorge's Sweet Corn down on King Road.

"Gotta have me some sweet corn to take home. It's the best there is," Grandpa said.

Which was true as true could be. The kernels were the size of marbles and sweet as sugar. You could even eat them raw.

"You could have done this on the way home, Grandpa. Why did you want me to come with you?"

"This isn't our only stop."

With bags full of sweet corn, they got back in the car and drove toward the Pink Kitchen Deli. Lucy didn't feel like talking, so Grandpa turned up the music again and sang along with Frank Sinatra. Lucy remembered a family dinner years ago when they'd been visiting from Chicago and Nonnina and Grandpa Miller had sung a big-band duet to wild applause.

And because Lucy was thinking and not paying attention to where they were going, she was completely surprised to find them turning down the same streets she'd ridden her bike on the day they went to the American Legion Auxiliary.

"Grandpa, no. It's okay. You don't have to yell at them."

"It's not okay. And I'm not going to yell at them. You are."

"What?"

"Well, I wouldn't advise yelling at anyone. But, listen, you can't let people like that chase you into a corner. Always say the thing that needs saying."

Lucy reluctantly followed her grandpa up the front walkway. He didn't even knock on the door, just let himself in.

The same men sat at the bar, even though it was only ten o'clock in the morning. Lloyd and Louis. Two names she would never forget.

"What can I do you for?" said Lloyd, the forgettable-faced man. Slowly, it seemed to Lucy, he recognized her.

"My granddaughter has something to say."

The two men turned to stare.

"Is that so?" Lloyd said.

Grandpa went on, "I'm not sure what your reasons are for turning away hard-fighting men who have served their country in Vietnam. A bunch of nonsense, whatever it is. But I'm especially hard-pressed to understand why you would turn away a little girl asking for help from men she considered to be heroes."

Lloyd's face didn't change. "Not everyone is a hero."

"You've got that right. Go ahead, Lucy."

Lucy had no idea what to say to these men who didn't care about her or her dad or anyone else but other World War II vets. She didn't understand what it might take for a person who had served in a war to turn away other men who served in different wars. It seemed to her they were all connected, *hitched to everything else in the universe*. Even if they didn't want to feel it.

The way she didn't want to feel her own connections to her family most of the time because big feelings could be hard to manage. And that made her mad at herself. And mad at these stupid men drinking beer at ten o'clock on a Tuesday morning, thinking they were better than her dad.

"My dad spent four years in medical school. And then another four years learning how to be a heart surgeon. And just when he finished at the top of his class and got a job, he was drafted into the army for a year. To serve as a doctor.

"He didn't ask to be deferred, like he could have. Because he knew that someone else would have to go in his place. And even though it wasn't reasonable—and was rather superstitious, actually—he felt like that would haunt him for the rest of his days.

"So, he left me and my mom. He left us for almost a year so he could save thousands of boys' lives. Young boys. Teenage boys. He lost an arm for it. And now he can't be a surgeon anymore."

It was hard for Lucy to breathe. The words were coming faster than she could think them through.

"And my friend? His dad is in Vietnam, too. And we found a Purple Heart that we want to return to a family who may or may not be missing their soldier. And all that seems more important than how you feel about Vietnam."

It could have been Lucy's imagination, but Lloyd didn't seem so smug. "You let one in, with their drug problems and their wild ways, you have to let everyone in. They aren't all like your dad."

The four of them stood there staring at each other. There was a dripping sound coming from behind the bar, and somewhere, the second hand of a clock ticked along its unstoppable way.

"Well, that's just terrible reasoning," Lucy said, spun around, pigtails flying, and walked out.

Grandpa and Lucy were quiet on the way home. Lucy was shaky, but feeling better somehow. She didn't even need to count her stones.

Grandpa drove the Lincoln into the driveway and turned off the ignition. He looked her straight in the eye. "When you look for all the reasons to keep people out, you will find them, Lucy. Look for the reasons to let people in. Look for the connections instead."

"Don't let Grandma take me," Lucy said.

"Never."

a wishing stone

*t*he phone rang early on Friday, waking Lucy on the morning she and Milo were to head over to Mac and Cheese's to sort through the sign-in books.

Brrrriiiiiingggg!

Lucy shot out of bed, heart racing at the unexpected alarm. It was hot already, the air outside Lucy's open window warmer than the air inside, so she closed it. She got dressed, placed the stones in her pockets and spritzed her Aqua Velva, all in a couple of minutes.

While she dressed, Dad murmured into the phone, the deep rumble of his voice floating down the hallway, if not the words themselves. More sounds. Morning sounds. Mom pouring water into the coffeepot. A cabinet door opening, then banging closed. Two coffee cups clanking together as Mom set them on the counter.

Then, silence. For too long.

Lucy padded down the hallway in her bare feet to find Mom and Dad standing perfectly still, staring at each other. Dad was pale and looked tired.

"What is it?" Lucy said.

Mom sighed. "Your dad didn't get into the Stanford cardiology program."

Lucy froze, feeling slightly nauseous. "Well, what do they know, anyway?"

Onetwothreefourfive-sixseveneightnineten.

"They know a lot, I'm afraid," Dad said, and shoved his hand in his pocket. His dark hair was mussed, as though he'd just woken up. He looked at the ceiling. "It seems I'm on to plan B."

"What's plan B?" Lucy said. "Can I help?"

Dad didn't answer. "I didn't sleep well last night. I think I'll lie down for a bit." He walked straight past Lucy into the bedroom and closed the door softly behind him. She caught the scent of his Aqua Velva. Or it might have been hers.

"Come here," Mom said. She patted the back of Lucy's chair at the breakfast nook table and then poured herself a cup of coffee. Mom's hair was slightly mussed, too, which was entirely unlike her.

Lucy sat down. She could still smell Grandma's Shalimar here and there, just as stubborn to leave as Grandma, it seemed.

"Are you sure you don't want to go stay with Grandma and Grandpa for a week or so? Grandpa's been itching to take you back to Lake Almanor for some trout fishing. I'm not going to force you. But I don't want you to stay here just because you think you should."

Lucy wasn't sure what she thought anymore. She only knew what she wanted. Lucy wanted things to be how they used to be. She wanted the first sound each morning to be Dad singing "Nessun Dorma" in the shower at the tops of his lungs instead of ear-popping silence. For the first thought of her day to be about what she would eat for breakfast instead of wondering if today would be the day that Dad would once again pull one of her ponytails and tell her she was his pie in the sky. For her troubles to be easy, like whether she should wear a blue sweater or a red one. She used to spend so much time picking out the right pair of socks to go with her outfits . . . Lucy found herself smiling.

"What's so funny?" Mom said.

"I'm just thinking about how much I used to love socks."

"You don't love socks anymore?"

Lucy shrugged. "I can't imagine caring about something that dumb ever again."

"I know what you mean," Mom said. She touched one of her pearl earrings. Mom had stopped wearing her Press-On Nails, impractical as they were, popping off all the time, and this made Lucy unbearably sad.

While Mom sipped coffee, Lucy stood up and got herself a bowl and some cereal.

"Pour some for me," Mom said.

They sat together eating spoonful after spoonful of Cocoa Puffs. Together, they slurped down the chocolate milk the cereal left behind. Lucy was fairly certain they had never slurped anything together in her entire life.

Over the year Dad had been gone, she and Mom circled around the big hole Dad left behind, as though they didn't know what to do with holes, or each other, maybe. They figured it out, though, little by little. Mostly by sticking to a rigid schedule, accounting for every minute. Mom had picked her up from school each day at precisely 3:05 and driven her home for a snack of peanut butter and fig jam on Ritz, while Mom sat beside her and they chatted briefly about their days. If there'd been a letter from Dad, Mom would wait to read it until Lucy came home. They cooked dinner together, Mom quizzing Lucy on fractions and recipe ingredients.

Every night after dinner, they read books. Sometimes they read to each other, sometimes in silence. If Lucy had a nightmare, which she faked sometimes, she'd crawl onto Dad's side of the bed and swear she could smell his Aqua Velva even though the sheets had been washed at least twenty times since he'd left.

Then they'd get up and start all over again. Day by day by day, Lucy supposed, they figured out, if not how to fill the hole of Dad's leaving, at least how to lean across it toward each other without falling in. Lucy didn't know what she would have done without her mother.

"Where are you in your hunt for the Purple Heart family?" Mom said.

"We're going to Mac and Cheese's today. They found all their sign-in books going back to 1960. We're hopeful we can find the person we're looking for."

Lucy still had a small niggling doubt about their sleuthing. After all, someone had buried that Purple Heart on purpose. For good reason, probably. But she also felt sure as sure could be, deep in her Rossi bones, that they had to find an answer. She bing-bonged between these two feelings over and over again until she thought she'd go crazy.

Mom nodded. "It's a good thing, what you're doing. And to be doing it with Milo. It's nice to see you have a friend."

"He's leaving," Lucy said.

"I know. Will he come back next summer?"

Lucy hadn't thought to ask. But even if he was coming back, that was a small consolation. He'd leave, and she'd be right back where she started when school began in September. She didn't want to start junior high spending her lunchtime in the library, and while Billy Shoemaker might respect her throwing arm, she was fairly certain he wouldn't be inviting her over for board games and pizza again anytime soon.

"Will we have to move again?" Lucy said. She tried to stay reasonable. Dad had to go back to school. This was a fact she couldn't change. As much as she was dreading the start of school, the idea of leaving was even worse. Her family. She couldn't imagine going back to a place where she had no family.

"I don't know."

"But we'll go with him, right? Dad won't go off by himself?"

"No, Lucy. We'll go with him."

Lucy couldn't stop thinking about the Mac and Cheese men. Dreaming about them. Wondering how a person might find it easier to be alone rather than stay with their family. She set her chin down on her folded arms and counted five grains of salt on the table. She pressed her finger down on each one, and they stuck fast like a constellation. "Why didn't we just move to Sacramento last year?"

Mom stood up and cleared their bowls. "What do you mean?"

"Grandma and Grandpa Miller are your parents. Why didn't we move to Sacramento to be near them when Dad left for Vietnam? Instead of here?"

Mom rinsed the cereal bowls and set them into the dish strainer. "You know how you just know things sometimes?"

For some reason, Mom's answer didn't surprise Lucy. "Yes," Lucy said. "Yes, I do."

"This is a better place for us."

Mom walked across the kitchen, her long legs showing through the slit in her robe. She took Lucy's face in her hands and gave her a half-smile. "But don't tell Grandma, okay?"

"Deal," Lucy said.

———

Lucy and Milo walked along Penitencia Creek to Mac and Cheese's place, Milo with another long stick commencing his usual pastime of beheading weeds. As the weed flowers hit the path, Lucy noticed acorns scattered here and there amongst the bushes and grasses of the woods. It was only mid-July, but those acorns were a reminder that fall was just around the corner, that Milo would be gone soon.

"Can I tell you something?" Milo said.

"Sure."

"Promise you won't get mad?"

Lucy narrowed her eyes. "I can't promise if I don't know what you're going to say."

Milo took a deep breath. "You sort of smell like my teacher last year, Mr. Matheson. He wore too much cologne."

Lucy laughed with abandon, like some force of nature had reached in and pulled it out of her. She bent over with it, bracing her hands against her knees. Her eyes watered.

"He was my PE teacher. He had pretty terrible BO, so he drowned himself in cologne to cover it up."

Lucy laughed even harder.

"Not that you have BO!" Milo said, and then, "Are you okay? It wasn't *that* funny."

So Lucy told him about her Homeostasis Extravaganza. How her comfort routine had helped her get through the days Dad had been gone. That she'd been spritzing Aqua Velva on herself for the past year and didn't even smell it anymore, if she was to be honest. Then she reached in her pocket and took out one of the stones.

"He sent them in his letters. This one is basalt with a quartz vein."

"A wishing stone," Milo said.

"It was the first one he ever sent. This is going to sound

crazy, but I felt a little bit like I was keeping him alive," Lucy finally admitted.

They both stood very still and looked at the small stone in the palm of Lucy's hand. She could hear the humming sound of dragonfly wings as they zigged and zagged along the creek beside them. For the first time, Milo didn't seem to notice them.

"Here," Lucy said, and held it out to Milo. "You take it. Until your dad gets home."

He took a step back, one hand raised as if to stop her handing it to him. "I can't."

"Why not?"

"I just can't. It's your lucky stone. What if something terrible happens?"

"I have nine more. Really. I want you to take it."

Lucy took hold of Milo's hand and put it in his palm. Then she closed her own hand around his. That was when Lucy noticed his eyes weren't just light brown, but the color of amber, that sticky stuff insects get trapped in. She had seen a collection at the California Academy of Sciences when her class visited last year. Milo even had small flecks in the amber of his eyes, like pollen stuck there for millennia.

"Thanks," he said, and looked away, shoving the rock into his shorts pocket.

They continued down the path toward Mac and Cheese's, Milo turning quiet. He stopped a few times along the way and looked right at Lucy, as though he wanted to tell her something, maybe. But then he just turned back toward the path and kept walking, kicking up dust, flinging his stick back and forth.

Lucy had given a great deal of thought to Mac and Cheese, how they could have been so careless as to send Lucy and Milo to the American Legion without knowing what they'd be in for. Because how could you trust people like that? Adults were supposed to know these things. But as she'd thought about it, Lucy realized a person could never be certain about other people. You could only be certain about yourself.

By the time they got to Mac and Cheese's, it was well past lunch, and a few men were standing around, talking. Lucy recognized the man in the wheelchair from the last time they'd visited. Doreen lay in the shade on the cement patio. Her head popped up when Milo crunched through the grass toward her. Then her ears went back and she trotted over, tail wagging.

"So glad to see you!" Mac called from the patio. He wore an army-green baseball cap, and reminded Lucy of a friendly-looking scarecrow now, rather than Icabod Crane. "We've got some volunteers to help out."

Beside him on the wall of the house was one of Gia's PICNIC FOR PEACE signs. Lucy figured Uncle G must have delivered it with the food from Dad's party.

Three boxes of sign-in books sat on the picnic tables along with lined paper and pencils. Mac introduced them to the men who were there. He apologized for what they'd gone through at the American Legion and VFW.

"I never thought they would have treated a couple of

kids like that. I'm truly sorry. But I heard you went back and gave them what for."

"Not sure if it did any good, but I sure felt better afterwards," Lucy said.

The man in the wheelchair's name was Clyde. His skinny legs were belted at the knees in contrast to his muscled arms and wide chest. "So, what, exactly, did you tell those no-good sons of a biscuit?"

"I told them about my dad losing an arm. And Milo's dad being in Vietnam right now. I told them they were being completely unreasonable," Lucy said. Because, to her, there was nothing worse on this earth than an unreasonable person.

They all clapped.

Which Lucy did not expect.

"I wish I could have been there to see that," Milo said.

Cheese came out of the house just then carrying a big plate of chocolate chip cookies and set them down. He gave a lopsided smile to Lucy and Milo. "Fresh baked. Help yourselves."

After they each grabbed a cookie, Mac brushed his hands together and said to Lucy, "What do we know so far?"

"Well, we know the name of the man in the pictures we found is Johnny, or I guess, John, and that his daughter's name is Amanda. The picture is dated 1963. We were thinking we should make a list of all the Johns that came through here during and after 1963," Lucy said.

They all got to work. Lucy could smell the dust as she turned pages, finding "John" to be an extremely common name. As her list grew, she became more worried that this was going to end up a big waste of time. And with Milo so determined, she feared he'd go back home without any answers. Then what? Would she wait for him to come back next summer and pick up where they left off? Would Lucy even be there next summer? Should she carry on with him in North Carolina and report her progress? Through letters? Lucy couldn't imagine doing this without him. She couldn't imagine not having him around every day.

"How long have you lived here?" Milo asked Mac, a pile of looked-through sign-in books growing beside him.

Mac closed the book he'd been working on and took another. He was easily a head taller than the rest of the men at the table.

"When my parents died, I inherited this big old rambling house, and since I never married, it just seemed like a waste of space. In the mid-sixties, I took notice of the Vietnam veterans and how they were having a hard time when they got back. I wanted to help. It grew from there. Rodney, or Cheese, as you know him, moved in in 1965."

"My dad would like it here," Milo said. "He'd wear a thick apron and barbecue all the meat. He'd tell loud, funny stories. Just like the ones he writes in his letters home."

"I bet he would, son," Cheese said. Only half his face worked for smiling, but that smile was so big and brilliant, Lucy almost didn't notice the half that didn't work. She imagined if she'd spent more time here, eventually, she wouldn't notice at all. Which made her think about how a person could get used to almost anything after a while, whether they wanted to or not.

Suddenly, that idea wasn't so frightening. What if these men could give her answers about her father? About what she might do to keep him from leaving? Lucy didn't know how to ask that question without giving away her own private fears, fears she preferred to keep hidden, even from herself sometimes. But then she thought about what she'd said to those men at the American Legion, how freeing it had been to speak her mind and heart.

Lucy swallowed and looked at a knothole in the wood of the picnic table. "So, my dad . . ." she started.

The chattering around the table went quiet.

"My dad isn't . . . doing very well. He lost his arm. He was a surgeon and now he has to start all over again."

Just then, Doreen sat up and placed her head on the bench between Lucy and Milo. Lucy scratched her ears and kept going. "I want to know . . . I need to know what I can do to make sure he doesn't leave."

Lucy wrangled all her courage and looked up at each of the men sitting around the table.

Mac, who was sitting closest to her, put his hand on her arm, just for a moment. Cheese steepled his fingers and stared at them as though they might hold the answer to her question. The other men didn't meet her eyes.

Lucy despaired—she'd clearly made everyone uncomfortable—and wished she could have sucked the words right back in.

It was Clyde who spoke up. "This is going to be hard to hear, kiddo. But there isn't one damned thing you can do to keep other people from doing their worst. It isn't fair and it isn't right. But it's the truth. And you've got to be brave enough to hear the truth."

Lucy didn't feel brave. But she supposed deep down, in the place where all her feelings about the war cooked and crushed, she knew what he said was true: there was nothing she could do about Dad. Except love him.

Clyde went on, "Maybe not today, and maybe not next week, you'll understand the gift in that. What kind of life would it be if all you did was try and make other people do what you wanted? You'd never have time for anything else."

Lucy didn't think that was much of a consolation at the moment, but she was glad she asked, even if the answer was hard to hear. It took about thirty minutes to go through the boxes and compile their lists. Once Mac and Cheese had removed all those Johns they personally knew and had talked to, there were twenty-six left. Of the twenty-six, seventeen didn't leave a forwarding address or phone number, which left nine names they could start with.

"There are only two here with phone numbers and seven who left street addresses and no phone number, none local except one in San Francisco, California," Lucy said.

"So, what's next?" Mac said.

"My school librarian, Ms. Lula, is helping. I called and she's trying to get some air force records for us. To see if she can find a roster for the Dirty Thirty," Lucy said.

"If we cross-reference the names, maybe we'll find the right John," Milo said while Lucy carefully folded their compiled list and put it in her pocket.

"Keep us posted. There are a lot of us who want to know how things turn out," Clyde said.

It was late afternoon by then, and more men had begun showing up in advance of the six o'clock meeting. By the time Lucy and Milo left through the backyard gate, there were two card games going on, and two men sat outside a canvas tent in folding chairs. A well-worn U.S. Army duffel bag sat at one man's feet, his whole world packed into that one bag, Lucy figured.

Both men wore bandanas around their foreheads holding back long hair. They saluted Lucy and Milo as they walked by, and Lucy suddenly saw her dad in their place, his whole world shrunk down to the size of a U.S. Army duffel bag, and worried, again, whether he might find that a relief.

Onetwothreefourfive-sixseveneightnine—

Lucy brushed against Milo's arm and counted that as ten.

the seventh dwarf

*a*fter coming up with their list of nine Johns, Lucy and Milo had to wait a few extra days for Ms. Lula to get back from her summer vacation visiting family in Los Angeles. Those days dragged on slow as a simmering marinara, so they were there, waiting for the doors to open when she returned at the end of July.

Ms. Lula's favorite part of her job at the Berryessa Branch of the San Jose Public Library was the question box. This was Lucy's favorite part of Ms. Lula's job, too.

The question box was a shoebox-sized, cherry-red box the librarians filled with the best questions the library patrons had asked, along with the answers they'd found.

What is that little plastic thing on the end of a shoelace?
An aglet.

Why do mockingbirds mimic other birds?
No one knows. But they don't just mimic birds. They are known to mimic dogs, bugs and even the hinge on a squeaky door.

What are the names of the seven dwarfs?
Grumpy, Happy, Sleepy, Dopey, Bashful, Sneezy and Doc.

Ms. Lula had told Lucy that she and her fellow librarians got the seven dwarfs question all the time. People would call in a frenzy and tell Ms. Lula they could only think of six names, gosh darn it, and they couldn't rest until they had the seventh dwarf.

"And it's always Doc. They always forget Doc," Ms. Lula had said.

Lucy understood this perfectly. Doc was reasonable and calm and didn't kick up a fuss, and so he was easy to overlook, she figured. Character traits she used to pride herself on having as well. But now she wondered what good it ever did anyone to be reasonable and calm and to never kick up a fuss. It just made a person forgettable, unhitched from everyone else.

"Darlin' Lucy!" Ms. Lula hollered as soon as she and Milo walked through the front door.

Ms. Lula was tall and lean and had a perfectly round Afro that was a shade darker than her skin. She had deep brown eyes like Lucy's, where you couldn't see the pupil unless you got extra close, and she liked to wear long, dangly earrings in all sorts of colors. Ms. Lula also had dark freckles across her nose and cheeks that she'd been teased about when she was younger. Right up until she mapped out all those freckles and declared herself to be a freckled version of the Milky Way and that she'd punch anyone who said any different. She was a gatherer of things, Lucy had noticed: inspirational quotes and zucchini bread recipes and sea glass in a jar on her desk. She'd gathered Lucy together when Lucy hadn't even realized she'd been in pieces.

Lucy was hit with an unexpected wave of gratitude at seeing Ms. Lula. In about three long strides, Lucy was in her musk-and-flower-smelling arms. "You've brought a friend!"

After the introductions, Ms. Lula said, "Boy, have I got some information for you. But first, let me see it."

Milo reached in his pocket and took out the Purple Heart. Ms. Lula looked it over. "This is the first time I've ever seen one up close."

"My father's looks exactly the same," Lucy said.

"You know why?" Ms. Lula motioned for them to follow her behind the desk and into a side room where there was a table and six large wooden chairs. In the middle of the table were three stacks of papers, and two hardcover reference books. "During World War II, the military was all set to invade Japan, and so they had thousands of Purple Hearts made in anticipation of the casualties. Instead, they dropped the bombs on Hiroshima and Nagasaki, which ended what was left of the war. So now there's a warehouse somewhere with stacks and stacks of Purple Hearts that I hope to goodness they'll never get to the bottom of."

Lucy was beginning to think the library wasn't the Giant Receptacle of Knowledge Ms. Lula had always referred to. The Giant Receptacle of Knowledge was Ms. Lula's own actual brain.

Milo was fidgety in his seat. "Did you find a register of the Dirty Thirty?"

"Now, what sort of librarian would I be if I didn't?"

Ms. Lula pushed a notebook toward Lucy and Milo, who had pulled two of the chunky wooden chairs to sit beside each other. Lucy leaned toward the notebook, and the vinyl seat wheezed.

"There was a total of sixty men in the Dirty Thirty, who served in two separate shifts, thirty men at a time, over twenty months. The first thirty pilots went over to help the VNAF, which is the South Vietnam Air Force. These were the first American men to fly in combat in Vietnam."

While Ms. Lula explained, Lucy took out the list of the names they'd written down from Mac and Cheese's sign-in books. She'd already given a copy to Ms. Lula, had read the names to her over the phone. They were hoping to find a match in her list of names.

"There! John Ruth!" Milo said. "He served in the second group of men from April until December 1963, and he also left a forwarding address with Mac and Cheese. In October 1964, he lived in San Francisco!"

"Yes, it's the only name on both lists. But here's the bad news," Ms. Lula said. "I couldn't find a recent phone book entry for John Ruth in San Francisco, or any of the surrounding areas. I even looked as far as Los Angeles. The military information I have is incomplete."

"Maybe he's dead," Milo said.

"It's a possibility," Ms. Lula said. And they all sat looking at the hard wood of the table, silent. Finally, Ms. Lula switched on an oscillating fan in the corner.

"Don't they keep track of the Purple Hearts they give out?" Lucy said.

"Some people have theirs engraved, but it doesn't look like yours has any markings, and the government doesn't track them," Ms. Lula said. She picked up a magnifying glass and looked over the Purple Heart more carefully.

"Well, that's dumb," Milo said.

"It's pretty dumb they don't track the names of people who receive the medal, that's for sure," Ms. Lula agreed.

"We have an address, at least. Even if it's old. Maybe he'll still be there," Milo said.

But Lucy had a feeling he wasn't. Deep down in her Rossi bones, maybe, she knew he wouldn't be there. Whether dead or just plain gone, Lucy wasn't sure. But she felt an emptiness inside herself. An emptiness she couldn't shake.

"Thanks for everything," Lucy said. "Really, everything."

She looked at Ms. Lula then, smack into her eyes. Ms. Lula reached across the table with both hands and held on to Lucy's. They were cool, her long fingers graceful. Lucy knew Ms. Lula played piano with those long fingers, had caught her in the empty auditorium one day playing the *Moonlight* Sonata after school. She'd told Ms. Lula everything that day. About her dad. Her trouble making friends. Her sadness. All of it.

"I knew you could do it," Ms. Lula said, and shifted her eyes toward Milo. "You only needed some time to figure things out."

It was then that Lucy really believed things could be different next year. Not only because Ms. Lula worked at the elementary school and Lucy was going on to junior high, but because Ms. Lula wasn't a twelve-year-old girl. She'd filled in the gap as best she could last year by feeding Lucy books and making her laugh and trying to soak up Lucy's loneliness. But it was up to Lucy now, to make a place for herself.

And Milo had shown her she could do it. She could make a friend.

"I will miss you, child," Ms. Lula said.

"I'll always visit," Lucy said, but she knew it wouldn't be the same. Because she didn't need Ms. Lula anymore, not in the same way she had last year. "You can't keep me away from books."

Ms. Lula stood and stretched her arms over the top of her head. "Get going, now. You two have some more sleuthing to do. And I want me some answers!"

Lucy and Milo walked back out into the lobby of the library, where the custodian was using a buffer on the beige linoleum tiles, back and forth, back and forth.

"Do you think we can take the train into San Francisco?" Milo said.

"I'll talk to Papo Angelo. He'll be heading into San Francisco soon for a meat run. He goes a couple of times a month. We can hitch a ride."

"It feels like we're running out of time," Milo said. There was a thin film of sweat on his forehead, and he swiped his arm across it absently. There wasn't any air-conditioning in the library, so the smell of books was thick and everywhere. Paper and dust and leather combined into a scent that was even better than Aqua Velva.

"We are running out of time. You're leaving soon," Lucy said.

Milo hung his head, and in Lucy's peripheral vision, she saw the heavy glass door to the library open, a small group of kids walk through.

Linda McCollam and two of the Dandelion Girls.

At first Lucy thought they'd walk right on by, but Linda stopped. "Heard you kicked Bernie Ryan's butt."

Which was not what Lucy had expected her to say.

"I sort of kicked all their butts."

"Cool. Who's the new kid?" Linda looked Milo over from fuzzy hair to hole-infested Converse.

"Milo. He's visiting for the summer."

"Shame it's only for the summer. He's cute."

Then she flounced all her long blond hair over one shoulder and winked at Milo, like she was Marsha Brady or something. Like there weren't enough boys who already thought Linda McCollam was drool worthy, she needed to bat her eyelashes at Milo, too.

But Milo didn't seem to notice. He was busy reading the flyers on the library bulletin board.

"We should bring a bunch of flyers to all the libraries," Milo said, completely ignoring Linda.

Seeing that her attention was going unnoticed, Linda flounced her hair over the other shoulder and walked toward her friends. "See ya around, Lucy."

Lucy gathered her nerve, and called, "Linda!"

Linda turned around.

"I'm sorry about what I said. About your cousin. Is he okay?"

She smiled. "He just got home three weeks ago." The other two girls who had come in with Linda—Susan and Winnie—rolled their eyes from where they stood. Winnie crossed her arms and tapped her foot. Impatient fluffs. "I'm sorry about your dad," Linda said, and fidgeted with the ribbon around her waist. "About lots of things."

Lucy noted that Linda was no longer wearing flaming mustard argyle socks but, rather, a pair of white flats and a seersucker dress. An outfit worthy of Audrey Hepburn. Grandma Miller would approve. She imagined Linda would have been impressed by Nonnina's fabulous clothes from the fifties, all tucked away in her closet. The cocktail dresses and the long gloves, the pointy heels and the dark sunglasses. She and Linda were probably too old, but Lucy imagined they could have had a spectacular session of dress-up.

Suddenly, Linda rushed over to the circulation desk and took a small piece of paper and pencil to scribble something down. Then she handed it to Lucy. As she fast-walked toward her impatient friends, she called over her shoulder, "Call me the next time those boys challenge you to a game! We'll both kick their butts."

Lucy looked down to find Linda had written her name and number on the little slip of paper. There was a heart over the *i* in Linda, which was silly and pointless and what sort of person drew a heart over the *i* in her name?

Linda McCollam, that was who. And maybe it was time for Lucy to stop thinking she knew so much about everything.

life is a lottery

*i*t was all set that Lucy and Milo would accompany Papo Angelo to San Francisco the following week to check on the last known address for John Ruth. In the meantime, Lucy and Milo papered the libraries all across San Jose with Milo's new drawings of the Dirty Thirty patch, the name they'd found and all the other information they had. They also stopped by Mac and Cheese's to update them and to ask them to spread the word.

As the days went by, Lucy became more and more anxious. The draft lottery was coming up on August 5, where Josh would find out his fate. Would he go away to college in the fall to become a veterinarian? Or would he be drafted into the armed forces against his will? She thought every day about what he'd asked her to do for Gia.

Lucy wasn't sure her heart could take it. She was already an overstuffed cannoli.

To make things even worse, Milo was only there for a couple more weeks, and Lucy found herself pretending he wasn't going anywhere, that he would move in with Mrs. Bartolo and summer would last forever. Lucy would gladly have put up with all the worst heat waves of summer combined for the rest of her life if it meant Milo and Josh could stay.

Somewhere in all that, Lucy finally relented and started watching *As the World Turns* in Mrs. Bartolo's cool house. After only a few days, she'd gotten sucked into the stories the way water gets sucked down a drain. Now she couldn't imagine her afternoons without them.

"They're all lawyers?" Lucy had said.

"Not all of them, just the Hugheses and the Lowells," Mrs. Bartolo said.

Lucy had become obsessed with the melodramatic lives of the people who lived in Oakdale, Illinois. Would Dan turn to drinking after seeing Claire get struck by a car? Would Liz recover from her nervous breakdown and get out of the institution? Would Betsy ever find out who her real father was?

She looked forward to sitting between Milo and Mrs. Bartolo on the green damask sofa, a cold glass of iced tea on a coaster in front of her, Mrs. Bartolo knitting with her nervous fingers, exclaiming, "Oh, no!" and "He deserved that!" every few minutes alongside the dramatic organ musical accompaniment.

Lucy looked forward to it perhaps more than she should. Because all those stories took her out of her own, if only for thirty minutes each day.

On August 5, when the soap was over, Mrs. Bartolo sliced a bunch of hot dogs in half and fried them in a pan. Once they were good and browned, she slapped those hot dogs between two slices of toasted white bread and served them up with potato chips. Lucy didn't expect much, but after one bite, she was sure this was the only proper way to eat hot dogs.

"Today's the lottery," Mrs. Bartolo said, digging into her own hot dog sandwich, which she'd covered in mustard. "Those poor boys."

Lucy nodded. "Uncle G is barbecuing, and Gia's boyfriend's family is coming over to watch so they can all be together."

"Sometimes it feels like life is just one big lottery drawing," Mrs. Bartolo said.

She looked at Milo, who was crushing his potato chips into tiny bits with the palm of his hand. He was quiet. The draft lottery probably got Milo thinking about his dad. And Milo never said a word about his dad, not how many days were left until he got home or what they were going to do when that happened. He was like a plane in a holding pattern in the sky where you can't land, but you can't go anywhere else, either. Lucy knew people had their own ways of dealing with hard things—her Papo Angelo carried Nonnina around in an urn, for gosh sakes—so she understood Milo's silence.

When Lucy finished her hot dog sandwich, she got up to look at one of Milo's bird drawings that Mrs. Bartolo had taped to the sliding glass door. It was a hummingbird. On the other side of the glass was a hummingbird feeder, and Lucy wondered if Milo had drawn it right there, watching those birds as they flitted from one small feeding tube to the next.

"Did you know," Mrs. Bartolo said, "that all bird species have a particular song?"

Lucy sat back down. "I didn't know that."

"A familiar melody that draws them a mate. So one bird sings, and another bird responds in recognition of their own kind."

They all turned to watch the birds in the trees outside, could hear their songs through the glass.

"Sometimes a bird will learn the wrong song. A sparrow will pick up the call of a finch. They don't know why. A fluke. Something wrong with their brains. But the bird will sing his heart out and never understand why the other birds don't come. Isn't that sad?"

Lucy looked at Milo. She wondered if he was thinking the same thing. That for all the ways they were different, Lucy and Milo learned the same song.

Later on, when Milo walked her home, they were quiet. Before she went up to her house, she stopped at the dragonfly garden, and she and Milo watched them zig and zag along the surface of the water in the early-evening sunshine dappling the creek. Blues and greens and yellows. Their iridescence reminding Lucy of Milo's drawings.

"They eat hundreds of mosquitoes every day," Milo said. "And since they only like healthy water, you can tell from where they live if the water is clean or not. Grams says all living things are interconnected that way. That we all have useful messages for each other if we just pay attention."

Lucy thought about that. About what sorts of messages she might give and receive without even knowing it.

———————

Josh Giovanioli was the oldest of three boys, and he and his whole family showed up at Uncle G's, Josh holding a lemon cake. Lucy answered the door because the rest of her family was already outside on the patio trying to enjoy what was left of the day before everything went sliding off in a new direction, whatever the outcome. She'd been in the kitchen fetching a Tab for Gia, who was a gloomy lump in a folding chair sitting next to Papo Angelo outside.

Lucy had changed into her tie-dyed dress when she got home from Milo's, and when she, Mom and Dad showed up on Uncle G's patio, Gia burst into tears and hugged Lucy. Gia had burst into tears two more times since then, once when Josh called to tell her they were running late, and once when Papo Angelo pulled up his own folding chair and sat beside her, pulling her head onto his shoulder. For the first time that Lucy could remember, Nonnina's urn wasn't right beside him. It sat on an end table next to the sofa in the house.

"Gia will be glad to see you," Lucy said.

Josh handed her the lemon cake. "I'll be glad to see her, too. But mostly for when this is all over, one way or the other."

Josh's brothers were eleven and eight and just as

gloomy-faced as his parents, who were both tall and had similar features, straight noses and wide-set eyes, which had showed up in each of their children. There was no mistaking they were related. So if Josh had to go away, there would be a reminder of him each time they looked in a mirror or at each other.

Dinner was tasteless, even though Uncle G cooked up seasoned rib eye steaks and Aunt Rosie made her famous macaroni salad. No one ate or talked much.

Lucy worried about Dad. He took Josh aside for a little while, talked to him quietly. She would have given anything to hear the words of comfort Dad was probably giving him. Or the facts, maybe. The cold, hard facts about what might be ahead. She watched them carefully, studied Dad's every move. He didn't look right to her. He was sad, just like the rest of them, and heavyhearted. But his coloring was off. Pale, even though he'd been spending time outside. And clammy, like he might be getting sick. Which sent a whole new batch of worries through Lucy's already overloaded mind.

Soon enough, it was time to move inside and turn on the television.

Mom and Dad sat on the love seat while Lucy sat on the floor between their legs. The room was silent.

The television screen turned blue, and the words *Special Report* flashed.

"And now, the draft lottery!" said a cheery voice that was totally inappropriate for the occasion.

Lucy looked over at Gia, who sat tall with her chin raised,

like she was ready to shout obscenities at the television announcer. She'd stopped crying and held Josh's hand in both of her own. The man on screen looked like a kid, no older than Josh. His job was to pull the small, lightweight balls out of the clear Plexiglas container that looked like an oversized fishbowl.

Uncle G had explained the way the televised draft worked to Lucy before it started. There would be two large containers on screen with little balls inside, light like Ping-Pong balls. In one container, birth dates were written on brown balls, and in the other, numbers from 001 to 366 were written on yellow balls. As a birthday was drawn out, a corresponding number was given until each day of the year was assigned, 001 through 366 because it was leap year. Then, next year, when it was time to bring in more troops, they'd start with those birth dates that corresponded with 001 on up until they had enough men.

Sort of like bingo. The prize being a trip to Vietnam.

The best they could hope for was that Josh's birthday wouldn't get called for a long, long time. Lucy had both her fingers crossed, and her legs, hoping he'd get number 366. They were decreasing the number of troops and had only taken all those boys with birthdates from 001 up to 125 last year. So as long as Josh's number was higher than that, he'd be safe.

Eventually, the boy on the television pulled Josh's birthday out of the container. April 16.

Lucy wished as hard as she could wish that the next ball would have a number higher than 125 because all those boys would be safe.

Josh's number was 023.

The room went still as Gia squeezed his hand.

He'd be going to Vietnam. Now it was just a matter of when.

Lucy watched as the Giovaniolis drove off in their wood-paneled station wagon to take Josh home, sad for all the unknown things to come. When would Josh's letter of induction come? Sometimes they came right away, sometimes not for months. Would Josh volunteer instead? Some boys joined the National Guard or other forms of service that would save them from the front lines.

But Lucy didn't think Josh would do that. He was like her father, thinking about the other boys he'd have to look in the eye or the ones who would have to go in his place. She used to think this was admirable, heroic even. But now she wasn't sure.

Dad went home, tired, while Lucy and Mom helped Aunt Rosie with the dishes. When that was done, Lucy went to Gia's room. The door was closed, and she could hear the soft melody of James Taylor. *I've seen fire, and I've seen rain. . . .*

Lucy knocked and let herself inside. Gia lay flat on her back on her orange shag rug right beside the record player. She was surrounded by stuffed animals. All Josh's carnival winnings since they'd started dating when Gia was thirteen. Just a year older than Lucy.

"I can't believe this is my life," Gia said. The song ended, and she sat up, put the needle back to the beginning and "Fire and Rain" played again. She flopped back onto the rug and looked up at the popcorn ceiling, forlorn.

Lucy knew there wasn't much she could do to help Gia. Gia would have her feelings—anger, grief, frustration—just like Lucy had. And she'd have to find her way through it, just like Lucy had. And no one, including Lucy, could look into her brain and give her what she needed. She'd have to ask.

The way Lucy could have asked. And didn't.

Lucy had been mad at Gia for a long time and realized that, in part, it was because Gia hadn't read her mind like a Fattucchiera and given her what she needed. Just like the Dandelion Girls at school.

How Gia chose to protest the war just didn't matter anymore.

Lucy lay down beside her on the rug and used a giraffe as a pillow. She took Gia's hand. She'd missed her cousin.

"I'm so sorry," Lucy said. Both for what was to come and what had already passed.

Gia cried then. Cried and cried like it was the end of the world.

Which, Lucy supposed, for Gia, it was.

one shining moment

*W*hen Papo picked Lucy and Milo up for their trip to San Francisco, Dad was still in bed. Since the draft lottery two days before, he'd started to run a fever. Mom tried to get him to go to the hospital, since he didn't seem to be getting better, but he kept insisting he was the doctor and knew what to do for himself. He had antibiotics and ten years' worth of medical training, so there wasn't any sense going into the hospital and having them tell him what he already knew.

Lucy didn't want to leave his side. He'd especially need her since Mom had to go to work.

"You are going to San Francisco today with Papo, and that's the end of it," Dad said. "We've talked about this. I don't need you hovering."

Lucy reached in her pocket and took out the small specimen of rose quartz Dad had sent from Vietnam. "It's a seven on Mohs' scale. It's supposed to help with circulation."

"There's nothing wrong with my circulation," Dad said, trying to hand it back.

"I'll feel better if you take it."

Dad closed his eyes and took a deep breath, holding the stone to his chest. "I'm sorry for snapping. I'll keep it right here all day. I promise. Now go. You have important work to do."

Lucy walked to the bedroom door, and before she let herself out, she turned back to Dad. "Will you tell me your love story? It will make me feel better."

Lucy wanted to hear about their chance encounter just then. She needed the reminder. That against all odds, people found their way to each other. And that knowing something deep in her Rossi bones was something she could trust.

"Papo is waiting. We can tell stories when you get home," Dad said.

Lucy quietly closed her parents' bedroom door and then put her hands in her pockets.

Onetwothreefourfive-sixseveneight . . .

———

Meat day was usually a glorious celebration of meat, when Papo Angelo would load up the overnight van with coolers of dry ice and drive into San Francisco so he wouldn't have to pay someone for delivery. He'd make a day of it twice a month, visiting relatives, eating lunch at Original Joe's and haggling the prices of his meat purchases.

Half of Lucy's extended family lived in San Francisco.

Her Big Papo Rossi, who had settled in the rolling hills of the Santa Clara Valley in order to grow his fruit, had a brother named Vito, who'd settled in San Francisco and opened up a fish store. And it was one of Vito's employees, Ralph Emeretti, who had married Great-Aunt Lilliana. Great-Aunt Lilliana still owned their little house in North Beach.

So Papo's first stop was always to Great-Aunt Lilliana's. Sometimes Great-Aunt Lilliana went with him on his journey to visit with relatives and haggle meat prices; sometimes she gave him espresso and biscotti, and sometimes she just sent him on his way. Always she gave him an earful of advice, a premonition if she was feeling generous. He'd often declared her the best big sister who ever was, but only when the other two sisters weren't listening, or he might find a chicken foot where he least suspected it. Like his coffee mug.

True story.

Lucy had gone with Papo Angelo on a few occasions while Dad had been in Vietnam to keep him company, sitting in flowered parlors and eating biscotti too heavy on the anise and patting the heads of many dogs and small children. She'd then go with Papo Angelo to Original Joe's and always ordered Joe's Special, a delicious scramble of eggs, hamburger, spinach and secret spices, which would throw Papo Angelo into fits of pretend offense because he'd never been able to talk the owner into divulging the "special" part of Joe's Special. Her most important job during these trips was to get Papo Angelo to stop haggling at just the right moment, just before the butchers would throw him out.

Lucy and Milo climbed into the bucket seats of Papo Angelo's white overnight van with the pop-up roof, and he shouted, "To the moon, Alice!" as he always did when the day was just beginning and there were mountains to climb or hills to conquer or just a nice chair in the shade to fall asleep in, depending.

Milo brought the flight helmet. Ever hopeful, figured they'd want that, too.

As they drove up 280 toward San Francisco, Lucy pointed out all the landmarks for Milo, of which there weren't many. There was Highway 92, which went up and over the hills to Half Moon Bay, where she had looked for the starfish on that day that seemed so long ago now, where they had the best milk bread in the entire world. Even Papo Angelo said so. She also told Milo about Uncle G going smelt fishing on Martins Beach and how he'd flash fry those fish right after they'd been caught and when he brought them to the deli, they sold out in five minutes.

"I miss Cleo's blueberry pancakes," Milo said.

"Who's Cleo?"

"He owned the U.S. Café in Fayetteville, and sometimes he'd give me and the guys a free breakfast, anything for the servicemen or their kids. We did all the grunt work for him in order to pay for it, 'cause we didn't want to take a handout. Carried in cases of things and unloaded them into the refrigerator. Poured syrup into those pourer things he had, with the little spout."

Milo watched the hillside go by, playing out his memories for Lucy.

"People would come and protest the war, sometimes," Milo said.

Which started Papo Angelo on a string of Italian mumblings. "You don't listen to the mindless idiots of the world," Papo Angelo said with gusto.

"You think Gia is an idiot?" Lucy said.

"I think Gia didn't know until now what she's been yelling about. It's different when you have something to lose."

"It's hard to ignore them when they're yelling in your face that your dad is a baby killer," Milo said.

"What did you do?" Lucy asked.

Milo half smiled, "We lit firecrackers and threw them off the roof into the crowd."

"I bet that felt good."

"Sometimes we'd all get together and go down with our own signs, cheering for the soldiers, our moms and dads. One time there was this lady, a loud one with all sorts of horrible things on her signs, and as soon as she saw us, she just stopped in the middle of a chant. She walked straight over to us. I thought she was going to yell, but she didn't. She just cried and threw her sign in the garbage. The protestors went home after that. They came right back a couple days later. But not her."

Lucy could see Papo Angelo watching Milo through the rearview mirror. He wiped at his eyes, because Papo Angelo was a feeler of feelings.

The fog was especially thick as Papo Angelo drove through the city to North Beach. Great-Aunt Lilliana lived in a two-unit peacock-blue jewel-box-shaped house on

Telegraph Hill that had a rooftop deck with views of the bay. It was a tiny little piece of heaven on earth, and Lucy loved it.

Lucy felt the pricks of the summer fog against her face as they climbed the stairs and Great-Aunt Lilliana welcomed them with kisses and how-are-yous and, of course, a bounty of food. She shouted, "*Mangiare e ingrassare*," to Milo, who smiled and dug in to the breakfast sausages, already used to being shouted at by Lucy's relatives, it seemed.

"I will meet you back here at four o'clock sharp," Papo Angelo said, pulling on his wool cap after he ate and had his customary espresso. "Good luck."

Lucy and Milo cleared the table and carried the dishes into the kitchen, setting them into the porcelain sink.

"So," Great-Aunt Lilliana said, "you've found the family."

"We hope so," Lucy said.

"You have. I have seen it. Wait here," Great-Aunt Lilliana said, and went into her spare bedroom, where she clunked things together, opened and closed drawers, and then Lucy heard an unmistakable clap and what sounded like a thousand wings all flapping at once. Then silence.

Great-Aunt Lilliana came back into the room carrying a small basket filled with herbs. She laid out two small pieces of black velvet. On each square, she laid a sprig of something green. "Rue," she said. "For protection on your journey. Now, pluck two hairs from your head."

Lucy closed her eyes. "Ugggghhhh."

"It's okay," Milo said. He plucked at his head with enthusiasm.

Even Great-Aunt Lilliana pulled on her own wild gray hair she ordinarily kept in a neat bun at the nape of her neck.

"Now we lay each hair on top of the rue."

Great-Aunt Lilliana stood up and went to the fireplace, scooping up a small container of ash, which she sprinkled over the rue and the hair. She then laid her hands, short-fingered, hard-working hands, over each small pile, mumbled and tied the ends of the velvet together with a length of thin black cord. She placed a pouch over first Lucy's, then Milo's head. Lucy felt herself resisting, denying. A thousand reasonable glass-shard thoughts tried to rip through her growing sense of hope. She didn't let them.

"Now. Close your eyes and envision your journey, what it is you want to find at the end of it."

Lucy finally let herself think about what she wanted. She wanted to find a whole family. A family who had survived.

When they'd each taken a moment, Great-Aunt Lilliana clapped one fierce clap and threw her hands up into the air, and Lucy willed her reasonable thoughts to fly up with Great-Aunt Lilliana's hands. For one shining moment, Lucy saw them hovering there, floating all around the ceiling, like bits of silver confetti.

In place of her reasonable thoughts, she let her heart lead the way.

an unexpected dragonfly

*i*t wasn't difficult to find 111 Clement Street. It was a tall building made of stucco that had been separated into apartments. Unit A was directly up a small flight of outside stairs and had its own entrance.

"You ready?" Milo said. He had the helmet under one arm.

"No. But this is why we're here," Lucy said, and held on to her pouch of rue for courage. It didn't matter that her legs were shaking. It didn't matter that she suddenly realized she had a lot of feelings riding on the answer to the question of whether or not this man was okay, or if he had left his family and buried the memory of them in the dirt.

And then it was happening. A woman with pixy-short dark hair and a crinkle in her nose when she smiled answered the door. She was thin, and Lucy suddenly wished she'd brought something for them besides the pictures. Biscotti, maybe.

"Yes?" the woman said. Not unkindly. Then she spied the helmet and her eyebrows furrowed in confusion.

Lucy couldn't find a single word.

"We're sorry to bother you," Milo said, and swallowed. "But we might have something that belongs to you."

"Does John Ruth live here?" Lucy found her voice.

The woman took a step back to call up the stairs. "Johnny!"

A teenager, short and burly, with a flat nose and a military haircut, hopped down the stairs to stand beside the woman. He resembled the Johnny in Lucy's picture, but couldn't be. The picture had been taken in 1963, almost ten years before. "Yeah? Who are you two?"

Milo and Lucy looked at each other. Milo said, "Is your dad here, maybe?"

The boy's eyes narrowed. "What do you know about my dad?"

The thin woman put her hand on Johnny's shoulder and stepped forward, slightly blocking him. Protecting him. "What's this about?"

Lucy took the plastic baggie out of her sweatshirt pocket and handed the three pictures to the boy. "We found these."

Before Johnny could get a good look at the pictures, the woman snatched them out of his hands, her eyes wide.

"Where did you get these?"

"Is that . . . Dad?" Johnny said.

Lucy hesitated. "We found them buried in a flight helmet in the hills just outside San Jose. Near Alum Rock Park."

Milo held out the helmet with the Dirty Thirty symbol

painted on the back, and Johnny took it. Then they all stood there, momentarily flustered, silent as the stars above.

"Heavens, look at us just standing here like a bunch of bumpkins. Come in!" the woman finally said. She opened the door wide enough for them to go inside.

"I'm Meg, and this is Johnny. Amanda!" Meg called, and a long-legged, almost-Gia-aged person came trotting down the stairs. She even had Gia's long, dark hair.

"Yeah?" She smiled at Lucy. She had the same crinkle in her nose as her mom.

"Let's all sit down for a minute and take a deep breath," Meg said.

Amanda looked confused, but followed her mom into the living room. Once they were all situated on the long velvet sofa and mismatched chairs, and introductions made, Meg took the three photographs and handed one each to Amanda and Johnny, keeping one for herself.

"It's Dad!" Amanda said.

"That was our last day together before he left for the war the first time," Meg said with a hint of a smile.

Milo took the Purple Heart from his pocket. "We found this, too."

Johnny leaned forward and took it from Milo. He looked at his mother. "I didn't know Dad was injured."

"He wouldn't talk about it. Even with me. Where did you find these things?"

"There's a house up in the hills that's a meeting hall sort of place for vets. They come together and tell stories.

Sometimes they stay overnight if they don't have anyplace else to go. We found the name John Ruth in the record books. He came through in January of 1965, and he left this address," Lucy said.

"Sounds like somewhere John would have gone. He was always off helping this vet or helping that one. Lord knows they weren't getting help from anyone else."

"So he came back?" Lucy said.

"For a little while," Meg said. She looked off toward the fireplace mantel where there was a folded American flag in a triangular box. "He came back the first time. But not the second."

Lucy and Milo both stared at the flag and without thinking, Lucy reached for Milo's hand. Lucy was heartbroken for this family, for herself. For Gia and Josh. For the whole wide world, it seemed. She hadn't realized how much she was counting on the idea that she would find whoever the Purple Heart belonged to. That she'd see a family who made it through the war whole.

"He didn't know how to be home. He couldn't sit still. He'd leave sometimes for days at a time. Finally, he told me he had to go back," Meg said. "That somehow, he hadn't done enough the first time."

"I'm so sorry," Lucy finally said. "I hope this hasn't made things worse."

"Heavens no, child. You haven't made things worse at all," Meg said. She looked young to Lucy, especially when she smiled. "We're happy to have whatever pieces of him we can get."

The helmet was a little dirty, but Milo had cleaned it mostly, so Johnny slipped it on, snapped the strap under his chin. Then he put both his hands on either side of the helmet, as though hugging it tight to his head. Maybe he was listening for something, the way you can listen to the inside of a seashell.

Lucy realized the Purple Heart wasn't just for the wounds of a soldier, but the family's too. A testament to their own resilience and bravery in surviving a different kind of wound.

"Mom, this is the first time I've seen myself this little," Amanda said. "Too bad we lost all the pictures."

Johnny looked at his folded hands. "They're in the spare room. In the closet up on the shelf behind a box marked *sweaters*."

"When did you find them?" Meg said, unsurprised.

"A few years ago. I was looking for a blanket to take to the beach."

"Why didn't you tell me?" Meg said.

Johnny just shrugged.

"What?" Amanda said, looking back and forth between her brother and her mom. "Mom, why did you hide them? And why didn't you tell me, Johnny?"

"We all have our own way of handling things, I guess. Some of us better than others," Meg said.

"Well, don't just sit there, Johnny. Go get them!" Amanda said. She took the Purple Heart from her mom and inspected it from top to bottom.

"I suppose it's time," Meg said. She looked at the flag in the wooden box over the fireplace. "Right, John? You found a way home, after all."

Lucy stood up, a bit wobbly on her feet, suddenly feeling like an intruder. "We should go."

Milo was still staring at the American flag folded in its triangular box.

"Can I at least give you something for your trouble? You must have been searching for a long time."

"No, ma'am." Milo stood up. "'You can't put a price on a good deed.' That's what my dad always says."

Meg stood up and gave them each a giant squeezy hug. Then Johnny came down the stairs with a fairly large box. Lucy hoped it was crammed tight with pictures. Amanda bounced up and down on the sofa, arms outstretched, ready to receive them.

After a few more thank-yous and Meg's insistence they at least take a small flag she kept with her pencils by the phone, Lucy hurried down the stairs and toward their bus stop without waiting for Milo. He tried to catch up.

"What's the matter?" Milo said.

"I don't know!" Lucy said. "I'm just so tired."

Lucy finally slowed down and they walked side by side over to Geary for the 38 bus to Union Square, where they'd pick up the 45 back to North Beach.

"I wanted him to be there, I guess," Lucy said. "I wanted to ask him questions. About the war. About how to keep your family together."

"But your family is together," Milo said.

How could Lucy explain that, somehow, they were together and not together at the very same time? That it didn't really matter if a body was next to you, if the heart was ten thousand miles away.

———

By the time they got back at four o'clock sharp, the fog had burned off. Great-Aunt Lilliana, Papo Angelo, Lucy and Milo went up to the rooftop deck for a few minutes to take it all in and say good-bye.

Great-Aunt Lilliana's rooftop was filled from front to back with flowers and bushes and different places to sit. She even had two small crape myrtles blooming their bright fuchsia hearts out. They all stood there quietly, watching the gulls dip and rise on the breeze, flying against the wind.

"I've booked the cruise," Papo said, hands shoved in his pockets. "We're leaving in October and hoping for clear skies and the aurora borealis. I've even purchased a backpack for Nonnina's urn."

"Why couldn't you have waited?" Lucy said, turning to look at Papo.

"For what, my Lucia?"

"You could have waited until we were all there to ring the bell for your last dollar. Why would you have done it when no one was around except Gia?"

Papo took a deep breath of salty air. His nose was pink. "Oh, Lucia. I have had that dollar for years."

"I knew it!" Lucy said. "So why *then*?"

Papo turned his hands out of his pockets and lifted them to the sky. "It suddenly came over me. *Now is the time!* And before I could stop and think, I just rang the bell like a ding-a-ling! I knew if I didn't do it just then, I might never do it at all."

Great-Aunt Lilliana turned to Milo and said, "Is it time for you, too?" Which surprised them all, including Milo. "Are you ready to show us what you're hiding?"

Milo didn't hesitate. He just took out the most magnificently carved dragonfly Lucy had ever seen. It was palm-sized and intricate and made of wood stained a dark red. Deep in his pocket all this time.

"It's a golden-winged skimmer," Lucy said, remembering his drawing.

Then, as though struck by lightning, or some other paralyzing force of nature, Milo slid into a heap. Lucy rushed to his side thinking he'd been hurt, or was having a seizure, or she didn't know what.

"What's the matter?"

Tears came down Milo's cheeks. "My dad's not coming home."

She wrapped her arms around his bony shoulders. "Oh, my gosh, why not? What happened?"

"He died," Milo said. "Three months ago."

"Three months..."

Lucy looked up at Great-Aunt Lilliana and Papo Angelo to see if they might understand what was happening. They both looked mournful, knowing. But of course they knew. Everyone probably knew except Lucy. Because she'd been so preoccupied with her own troubles. Papo leaned down and put a hand on Milo's shoulder.

Great-Aunt Lilliana left them huddled there and went downstairs. She came back with a handkerchief, a glass of water and a baby aspirin. She also carried another herb of some kind. By the time Great-Aunt Lilliana tied the pouch around Milo's neck and put her hand over the pouch and his heart, Milo was still.

"I wanted to tell you a hundred times. But I just couldn't say it out loud," Milo said. He looked at Lucy. "We got his Purple Heart in the mail. In the mail! They didn't even deliver it in person. And I was so mad. About all of it. And so I took it out to the Cape Fear River . . . to the place I'd drawn the dragonflies with Dad. I took it out there and I . . . I just threw it . . ."

Milo couldn't finish. He cried instead, and Lucy held him tight. She was sick for his loss, sad because he hadn't trusted her sooner.

And astonished because this journey hadn't just been hers.

It had been Milo's, too, of course.

They were a team.

pieces of forever

On the way home, Lucy didn't let go of Milo's hand. Papo played an eight-track tape of the Beethoven Lucy loved so much. She hoped it was soothing for Milo, too.

They each looked out their windows, in opposite directions, as the setting sun tinted everything orange. Lucy wondered if she should have asked Milo more questions about his family over the weeks they'd been getting to know each other. She'd felt something was off, deep in her Rossi bones, but had been so caught up in her own troubles that she hadn't pushed him, asked for more. Hadn't really made herself a comfortable place to land for Milo, like the swamp milkweed he'd planted for the dragonflies.

But what if Milo's attempt at homeostasis had been to hold everything in?

Lucy thought about what she'd figured out for herself. That you had to ask for what you needed. No one was a mind reader. Not even Great-Aunt Lilliana.

At first, Lucy had wondered why her family hadn't told her about Milo. Uncle G, Great-Aunt Lilliana, Papo Angelo. Her memories clicked together like puzzle pieces and she realized they had all clearly known. But then she remembered what Uncle G had told her when she'd asked about Milo earlier. He'd said it was Milo's story to tell, and Milo's alone.

Lucy then thought about what she and Milo had done together this summer, how different it may have been had they told her. Would she have treated him differently? Would their friendship have been shadowed by grief? She would never know for sure. But she was glad for the way things turned out. Serendipity, she was certain, had been with her this summer. Would be with her always now that she understood what it meant.

———————

Lucy knew something was wrong the moment she stepped inside the front door. The empty house, the absence of heartbeats or breathing, was something Lucy could feel deep in her Rossi bones. Papo Angelo and Milo were right behind.

"Mom? Dad?"

It was still daylight, just past six o'clock, and Milo hadn't wanted to go home just yet. He figured Mrs. Bartolo would take one look at him and know he'd finally told Lucy the truth, something she'd been trying to get him to do for a while now, he'd said. Then she'd cry, and Milo just wanted a little more time before all that happened.

Milo stepped toward the phone to call Mrs. Bartolo and

let her know they were back. "Hey, Lucy, there's a note here." He handed it to her.

Dear Papo and Lucy,

Uncle G had to take Dad to the hospital.
We're at Stanford. Come when you get home.

Love,
Mom

Lucy's worries and fears, every single terrified thought she'd ever had while Dad was gone, came flapping back all at once, like the heavy beat of bird wings against the inside of her head. She shoved her hands into her pockets to count her stones, but they didn't do anything to help calm those thrashing, thumping thoughts.

She rushed into her parents' bedroom to fetch the stone she'd given Dad earlier, mad at herself for having left it behind. And for giving one to Milo. What if her stones only worked if they were together? What if she'd broken whatever sort of safety spell had knitted itself around them?

Now she really sounded like Fattucchiera. Next she'd be searching for tomatoes and a willing belly button to put them on. She had to take deep breaths. She had to be reasonable.

The stone wasn't on Dad's nightstand.

"Lucia," Papo said from the doorway, "get a sweater. It might be cool in the hospital."

Right. A sweater. She rushed into her room and grabbed the nearest one hanging toward the far right side of her closet.

A red cable knit she'd outgrown last year, but she didn't want to waste any more time searching for something that fit. On her way out, she picked up the photo of her and Dad sitting on her nightstand, alone now that the *Johnny and Amanda* pictures were back where they belonged.

"I called Grams," Milo said when she came out of her room. "I'd like to go with you."

Lucy couldn't find the right combination of words to reply, so she just took his hand again.

Papo Angelo shooed them out of the house, where they climbed back into the overnight van, alongside all the coolers of meat, which would surely go bad, and zoomed off into the early-evening dusk.

When Dad was sending the stones in his letters, Lucy had looked up the cycle of rocks in her *Encyclopaedia Britannica*. Igneous, sedimentary and metamorphic. Igneous rocks, like Half Dome in Yosemite, would crumble into bits over thousands and thousands of years and then those bits would break some more, pounded by wind and rain and furious storms until they were nothing but tiny particles, buried, but not gone. Because deep inside the earth, the forces of pressure and friction went to work on those tiny bits and eventually turned them into metamorphic rock and then more heat and pressure turned them igneous, which would push through all that earth and rise again, strong and true. Over and over, the cycle would continue until the end of time. Lucy liked the idea that she carried little pieces of forever in her pocket.

As they walked into the front vestibule, a teenager with a pink candy striper dress and square nurse's hat to match directed them where to go. It was almost the end of visiting hours.

Lucy took a moment to imagine the life she would have had if Dad had come home whole. She would have walked through these echoing hallways to visit her father while he was tending patients, maybe, bringing him dinner like she and Mom had so many times before.

And then she let it go. She let it all go. Whatever they had been, whatever they had hoped to be, was truly gone.

Gone with Dad's arm.

But that didn't mean they were doomed.

It didn't mean anything other than they had to start over.

And starting over was hard.

Uncle G sat in the Pine-Sol-scented waiting room, still reading *Catch-22*. The small sitting area had windows on three sides. He stood up as they walked in, and Lucy flung herself into his arms quite unexpectedly. "Is he going to die?"

"What? No! No, of course not. There's an infection that settled into his stump. They may have to go in and take a little more of the bone. But he's okay. He'll be okay."

Lucy would only believe that when she saw him with her own two eyes. "Can I see him?"

"One at a time," Uncle G said.

Without a word, Papo and Milo sat down in the

scratchy-looking beige chairs. They were both pale. Papo settled his arm around Milo's shoulder.

Nurses bustled around in their white dresses and matching stockings, on the phone, going in and out of rooms, their shoes squeaky against the shiny linoleum floor.

Uncle G knocked on the large wooden door and opened it without waiting for an answer. Dad sat in the hospital bed, propped up, with an oxygen mask over his mouth and nose. He was pale and clammy, like he'd been the night of the draft lottery, which seemed like ages ago. His eyes were closed.

Mom sat in a chair beside the bed, her hand wrapped around Dad's. She brushed away a tear and motioned for Lucy to come in. "He's okay," she said.

Lucy leaned against Mom's legs, half sitting in her lap, and stared at her dad.

"I'm going to get some coffee," Mom said. "You stay. Keep your dad company."

Dad opened his eyes and seemed to focus on the pinpricked ceiling tiles. Then he turned his head and looked at Lucy. He moved his hand toward her. The piece of rose quartz rested in his palm. She took his hand, the stone nestled between them.

Mom and Uncle G left quietly.

Lucy didn't know what was happening inside her. It felt like fireworks and bird wings flapping and an earthquake of emotions, all of them tumbling so she couldn't focus on any one in particular. So, she closed her eyes, took a deep breath and sifted through them all until she found the one lurking thing she'd been most afraid of for all those days and nights Dad had been gone. The thing that was still true now, if he didn't take better care of his arm.

"You could have died," Lucy said. A whisper.

"But I didn't. I'm right here," Dad said, muffled through the oxygen mask.

"I'm scared," Lucy went on. "I don't want to be scared anymore."

She flopped down into the chair and leaned forward, resting her forehead on the clean white sheet. After a moment, Lucy felt Dad's hand on the back of her head.

"Don't be scared. I'm right here," he said.

Lucy wanted to believe that more than anything. But she didn't. He was still off somewhere else, living through the war, or the explosion, or whatever else was going on in his mind each day, carrying him away from her. From their family.

"You're not. You're not here at all," Lucy said, muffled by the sheet.

"I'm trying, Lucy. This is just what trying looks like right now."

"Well, it's not looking very good."

Eventually Lucy sat up as Dad adjusted himself in the bed, smoothed the sheets. "I suppose you're right about that, considering where we are."

When Lucy had found out Dad was going to Vietnam and that she and Mom were moving from Chicago to San Jose without him, she'd gone into her closet and wouldn't come out. She had supplies: a giant thermos of water and eight peanut butter and jelly sandwiches. On the first day, her friend Trina had come over and stayed in the closet with her. Mom told them both they were being overly dramatic, but for once, Lucy didn't care.

Lucy remembered the angles of her mom's elbows, hands propped on hips, her look of utter dismay and confusion.

Once Mom left to go pack more boxes, Trina said, "Next time she puts her hands on her hips like that, just pretend she's about to do the chicken dance. It makes all moms less scary."

Lucy and Trina made long intricate plans about running away. They had an itemized list. They affixed bandanas to the ends of two yardsticks and figured they would head to the nearest train and go wherever the winds tumbled them.

Later that night, both moms stood outside the closet, hands on hips.

"You come out of there right now, Trina Fatulli!" Mrs. Fatulli said.

Trina and Lucy tried unsuccessfully not to giggle at their inside joke about the chicken dance, which just made both moms angrier. The girls still refused to come out.

Until Dad came home.

Then Trina skedaddled. Only instead of Dad insisting Lucy do the same, he crawled inside and sat beside her.

"You've fallen off the horse," Dad said.

"I don't want to go to San Jose now."

"Of course you don't. Why would you? Your friends are here. Your school is here. But go you must."

Lucy had laid her head in Dad's lap. She knew it was true. So she made him promise, again, that he'd come back from Vietnam, even though she knew it was a promise he couldn't make then. But it was a promise he could make now.

She looked at her dad lying in a hospital bed and said the only thing that really mattered to her.

"You promised you'd come back to me."

Finally, after what seemed like forever, as the clock ticked on the wall, and the nurse's shoes squeaked against the hallway floors outside, Dad took a long, shaky breath. "I will, my Lucia. I will."

Lucy laid her cheek against the sheets again, comforted for the moment, and Dad rested his hand on her head again. They sat like that for a long time.

"Now will you tell me your love story?" Lucy said, hopeful.

Lucy needed to hear that, even against the greatest of odds, family always found their way to each other.

"Why don't you climb up here beside me? It's a long story, you know," Dad said.

Lucy knew.

strong and true

*i*t wasn't a long story. Dad just liked to tell it that way.

They'd met during a fender bender, Mom and Dad.

Mom was on one corner of the sidewalk on a blue-sky spring day, wearing a butter-yellow dress and a sun hat, waiting to cross the street and catch a bus to Foothill Junior College, where she was taking a business course. Lucy had always pictured her there wearing her signature red lipstick, a breeze flapping her skirt around so that her knees were showing.

Dad was on the other corner of the sidewalk, waiting to cross to the opposite street, where he was meeting some friends to study in a nearby coffee shop. Lucy had always pictured him there smoking a pipe, even though he didn't smoke, with an arched eyebrow and wearing a sweater with elbow patches like Mr. Rogers.

Then there was a loud bang!

Because a snow-white Chevy plowed into the back of a red Thunderbird right there in the middle of the intersection. Both Mom and Dad were startled on their respective corners, Mom's hand flying to her mouth, Dad dropping his pipe. Then, because they were both spectacular people who cared for the welfare of others, they flung themselves off their corners toward the crash to see if they could help. Dad opened the driver's-side door at the exact moment Mom opened the passenger door, and there, right in front of the stunned faces of the accident victims in the red Thunderbird, they fell in love.

When Dad was being silly, he'd say she was a virus he couldn't shake. When he was being romantic, he'd say she was his Penelope from Homer's *Odyssey*.

Which Lucy knew inside and out because Dad used to chase her and Mom around their Chicago apartment, shouting quotes at them from Homer. He told them those quotes made him feel powerful and brilliant and ready to take on the world:

> *By hook or by crook this peril too shall*
> *be something that we remember!*

He'd chase them until they all fell on the sofa in fits of laughter. Lucy never understood most of the quotes Dad used to shout, but what she did understand about *The Odyssey* was that the hero, Odysseus, spent twelve thousand, one hundred lines of dactylic hexameter to get back home to his Penelope.

In some ways, Dad was still on a journey back home. It was just taking a little longer than they expected.

Lucy figured she could wait.

———

The Picnic for Peace at Happy Hollow Park over Labor Day weekend started with a bang. A literal bang. Great-Uncle Lando had bought leftover fireworks from the same guy that sold him the New Year's Eve party favors. Great-Uncle Lando was always one party behind the rest of the world.

It was called a Jet Dragon Snake, and as it flew off into the sky, breaking about every ordinance the park had set up for their Picnic for Peace, Lucy froze in place, taking a quick sideways glance at Dad, who was also, most likely, not fond of explosions. But he didn't seem to notice much or, if he did, kept it to himself.

The whole family was there, just like at Dad's Welcome Home party. There were blankets in all the colors of the rainbow lying flat in the grass with various relatives sitting, standing and eating. Of course, Great-Uncle Lando had set up the bocce balls, and the Hairy Uncles played with all the kids. The smell of barbecue was in the air, and a band had set up on a portable stage, the rickety kind you see at weddings. They played the Beatles and James Taylor not very well. But they tried.

Milo was there. Without any warning, his mom had showed up about a week after Dad came home from the hospital. She'd driven all their things across the country with Lola, their German shepherd. They were starting over and living with Mrs. Bartolo for a while.

Lucy had been with Milo when his mom drove up and opened the passenger door. Lola made a beeline for Milo, knocking him flat in Mrs. Bartolo's front yard, licking his face while Milo yelped helplessly and wrestled with her in the grass for a good long while. His mom, whose name was Mandy, held on to Milo for five solid minutes. They just rocked back and forth in each other's arms.

Mandy, Milo and Mrs. Bartolo were right beside all the Rossis at the Picnic for Peace. Josh was there with Gia, the two of them in their own little world, whispering to each other, making plans. Josh had decided to sign up early since he'd drawn such a low number in the lottery. Plus, Italians, he'd said, got sent to the front lines, so he was hoping that by volunteering, he'd get a better placement. He was reporting for the army's boot camp in three weeks' time. Lucy didn't know how she'd get through it all again, but she would be there for Gia, no matter what.

For now, Mom, Dad and Lucy weren't going anywhere. Dad had decided he needed to heal and take the time to figure out what he really wanted to do. He had many ideas, like being a pediatrician, or maybe working in health care for veterans, and figured he could volunteer his time until he found the perfect fit.

As the sun went down and the stars came up, Dad called Milo over to their blanket.

"Here," Dad said, and handed him his Purple Heart. He had already run the idea by Lucy. "Until your dad's replacement comes."

Lucy thought for certain Milo wouldn't take it. But he did. "Thank you, sir. I'll keep it safe."

"I know you will."

Many people spoke that night. About peace. About connectedness. About how we would all get through this together, and Lucy felt they were speaking directly to her, and speaking true. She took comfort in those words in a way she hadn't been able to while Dad was gone.

Linda McCollam was there, as well as Billy Shoemaker and some of the kids whose butts Lucy had kicked in Crazy Kick Ball Tag. Lucy was able to introduce Milo to the kids she'd gone to school with last year. Kids she hoped to call friends one day soon. School was starting this week, and with Milo by her side, she was ready. She figured she would have been ready even if Milo had gone back to North Carolina, but having him there was a bonus. Like finding an extra prize in the Cracker Jack box.

After a while, Lucy ended up back on their blanket beside her father, as she knew she would. Periodic checkups, she figured, weren't so bad, and who could blame her, really? It would take all of them a little time to sort things through.

While the ruckus of the night went on around them, Lucy and Dad lay back on the blanket and looked up at the stars.

"Look," Lucy said, after she'd correctly named Orion's Belt. "It's the Joes."

Dad pointed to the Big Dipper. "Uncle Lando's Pink Champagne Ladle."

"Aunt Lilliana's Premonitions," Lucy said, pointing to Cassiopeia.

And so they went, naming the constellations as they always had.

When she considered the moon, she didn't think of her dad anymore, pulling the tides and keeping the earth on its axis. She thought about the fact that the moon was a giant stone in the sky, and would forever remind her of her Homeostasis Extravaganza, and the summer she met Milo Cornwallace.

Lucy still carried her stones, not yet ready to let them go. She thought about the rock cycle often, knowing she was right where she was supposed to be—with the people she loved most in the world.

While Dad had been gone, Lucy figured she'd been trapped in the metamorphic stage of things, feeling her heart harden from the pressure, transformed into something she didn't recognize. But really she'd just been getting tougher without knowing it. While Dad had been gone, she'd been turning igneous so that, eventually, she'd rise again, like Half Dome.

Strong and true.

author's note

W hile Mac and Cheese's home in San Jose, California, isn't a real place, many places like this did exist as the Vietnam War progressed. By 1971, the year in which the book is set, the sentiment of many in the United States had turned against not only the war itself, but the military personnel fighting in it. As in all wars, the fighting was ugly, but unlike previous wars, camera crews were on the ground in Vietnam and captured events as they happened. Certain footage chosen to be shown on the news made people angry and sewed division. Even organizations meant to support veterans and their families weren't sure how to move forward. Some posts within the American Legion and the Veterans of Foreign Wars turned Vietnam veterans away because of the perception that they were drug addicts and murderers.

Post-traumatic stress disorder is, as defined by the

Mayo Clinic, "a mental health condition that is triggered by a terrifying event—either experiencing it or witnessing it. Symptoms may include flashbacks, nightmares and severe anxiety, as well as uncontrollable thoughts about the event." But this terminology didn't exist at the time of the Vietnam War. Anthony Rossi, Lucy's dad, was certainly suffering from this when he came home, along with many of his fellow veterans. But there wasn't help for them at the time. Flashbacks and severe anxiety made it difficult for men to adjust to life back in the States with their families. The behaviors derived from these symptoms were a large part of the reason the American Legion and Veterans of Foreign Wars decided to turn them away. The problems were just too great, and these organizations were not equipped to handle the many and varied psychological needs of the Vietnam veterans when they came home.

Also, the men coming home were very young. Because of the draft, many men serving in the war were between the ages of eighteen and twenty-four. Men could receive a deferment, or a delay in service, for going to college, working in an industry that helped the war effort, being the head of a family or having a physical ailment that prevented them from serving. But not all men. Most who were given deferments were in the upper classes, leaving the poor and minority communities to serve.

The draft happened the way it did in the story, once per year from 1969 to 1972. Induction through the draft ended in June 1973, and the war ended on April 30, 1975.

The way the draft worked was by pulling birth dates and corresponding numbers from 001 to 365 (366 in 1972, a leap year). Then, each of the birth dates would be placed on a large board beside their corresponding number. In 1971, the year of the story, Josh Giovanioli's birth date pulled number 023. He, along with every other person whose birth date corresponded with the numbers 001 through 095, would have been called for service in 1972. The table below shows how many birth dates were called each year for service. On the following page is a table where you can look up your own birth date to see if you would have been drafted into the Vietnam War along with Josh in 1971.

SERVICE YEAR	DATE OF DRAWING	ADMIN. PROCESSING NUMBER (NO. OF BIRTH DATES DRAFTED)
1970	December 1, 1969	195
1971	July 1, 1970	125
1972	August 5, 1971	095
1973	February 2, 1972	095

SELECTIVE SERVICE SYSTEM
1972 RANDOM SELECTION SEQUENCE, BY MONTH AND DAY

	JAN	FEB	MAR	APR	MAY	JUN	JUL	AUG	SEP	OCT	NOV	DEC
1	207	306	364	096	154	274	284	180	302	071	366	038
2	225	028	184	129	261	363	061	326	070	076	190	099
3	246	250	170	262	177	054	103	176	321	144	300	040
4	264	092	283	158	137	187	142	272	032	066	166	001
5	265	233	172	294	041	078	286	063	147	339	211	252

(continued on next page)

(continued from previous page)

	JAN	FEB	MAR	APR	MAY	JUN	JUL	AUG	SEP	OCT	NOV	DEC
6	242	148	327	297	050	218	185	155	110	006	186	356
7	292	304	149	058	106	288	354	355	042	080	017	141
8	287	208	229	035	216	084	320	157	043	317	260	065
9	338	130	077	289	311	140	022	153	199	254	237	027
10	231	276	360	194	220	226	234	025	046	312	227	362
11	090	351	332	324	107	202	223	034	329	201	244	056
12	228	340	258	165	052	273	169	269	308	257	259	249
13	183	118	173	271	105	047	278	365	094	236	247	204
14	285	064	203	248	267	113	307	309	253	036	316	275
15	325	214	319	222	162	008	088	020	303	075	318	003
16	074	353	347	023	205	068	291	358	243	159	120	128
17	009	198	117	251	270	193	182	295	178	188	298	293
18	051	189	168	139	085	102	131	011	104	134	175	073
19	195	210	053	049	055	044	100	150	255	163	333	019
20	310	086	200	039	119	030	095	115	313	331	125	221
21	206	015	280	342	012	296	067	033	016	282	330	341
22	108	013	345	126	164	059	132	082	145	263	093	156
23	349	116	089	179	197	336	151	143	323	152	181	171
24	337	359	133	021	060	328	004	256	277	212	062	245
25	002	335	219	238	024	213	121	192	224	138	097	135
26	114	136	122	045	026	346	350	348	344	069	209	361
27	072	217	232	124	241	007	235	352	314	098	240	290
28	357	083	215	281	091	057	127	037	005	010	031	174
29	266	305	343	109	081	196	146	279	048	079	230	101
30	268	---	191	029	301	123	112	334	299	087	014	167
31	239	---	161	---	018	---	315	111	---	160	---	322

* *Table pulled from the Selective Service System government website at sss.gov.*

acknowledgments

To the people who kept me sane on a monthly basis: Georgia Bragg, Leslie Margolis, Anne Reinhard, Christine Bernardi, Victoria Beck, Edith Cohn and Elizabeth Passarelli. I'm not sure how I'd do this without you guys cheering me on.

To this list, I must add Nan Marino, who was always at the end of the phone, or text, giving reassurance that I would, indeed, survive the writing of my second book. And third. And maybe even my fourth and fifth.

Stacey Barney and Rosemary Stimola, a talented twosome if ever there was one. Batman and Robin, Rogers and Astaire, Abbott and Costello—they've got nothing on you. Thank you for reading so deeply and helping me find the story. I would not have gotten it all together without your careful tending.

I'd also like to thank my childhood Italian family, who

made things bearable and gave me so much material to work with. And my adult family, Kevin, Kate, Sara and Maddy. Thank you for putting up with my long journeys into night. You are my everythings.

Turn the page for
a sneak peek of Tracy Holczer's

THE SECRET HUM OF A DAISY

She's on a journey home—
but she doesn't know where it will lead her.

THE SECRET HUM OF A DAISY

TRACY HOLCZER

1

Two Hundred
and Fifty-Six
Mississippis

All I had to do was walk up to the coffin. That was all.
I just had to get there and set the gardenia on the smooth
brown wood. Grandma said gardenias were a proper funeral flower. As if there was such a thing.

But my mind kept turning to daisies. The wild ones
I'd found and stuck into the cold white funeral wreaths.
Mama would have liked that. She'd told me that daisies
spoke in a kind of song, a secret humming that birds could
feel in their hollow bones, drawing them close. She said I
could feel it, too, if I tried, along the fine hairs of my arms
and neck. That we all have a little bird in us somewhere.

But there wasn't any bird in me. I could never hear the
daisies either. Or any other flower for that matter.

Listen, Grace. Mama's voice seemed to drift near the
stained glass windows where wet snow stuck and then slid
down the colored panes.

Grandma told me it had been a cold winter and it
wasn't over yet, even though it was April. One of the only

facts she'd shared with me since we'd met the week before. Of course, it wasn't like I knew how much it snowed here or when, being from just about everywhere else. In all our wandering across the great state of California, Mama had never mentioned the Sierra Nevadas or her hometown, Auburn Valley.

Grandma took my hand in her damp one and squeezed. Hard. "Listen, now," she said.

I pulled my hand out of hers with a juicy *plop* and wiped it down my skirt.

". . . she was a loving mother," said Pastor Dave, his voice turning from buzzing to words. More words like "free spirit," "quick to laugh," "full of life." Grandma fidgeted in her seat. Other people fidgeted too. I wondered if they'd known Mama years ago.

Then Pastor Dave said God took her for his own reasons.

But it wasn't God; it was the river.

I closed my eyes and pushed those thoughts away. Thoughts about Mama's last night, what I might have done different. Thoughts about Mrs. Greene and Lacey and how they were more of a family to me than Grandma would ever be. I turned around to find them at the back of the church, still fuming at Grandma for not letting them sit here in the front row with us. But just the sight of Mrs.

Greene, her quick nod of confidence, gave me the courage to do what I had to do.

Pastor Dave stopped talking when I stood up.

I stared down at my too-tight Mary Janes, skin puffing around the edges like marshmallow. Twelve was too old for those dumb shoes, but they were the only decent ones I owned. They squeaked as I stepped toward the giant sprays of sweet white flowers, eyeing the wild daisies I'd tucked in around the bottom.

There was a gasp. Or maybe it was my shoes.

Pastor Dave cleared his throat and picked up where he'd left off. Pews creaked, nylons hushed. I felt eyes on my back like a heat. I turned around to face those eyes, to look at Grandma, hard as the bench she sat on, daring her to stop me, but she was staring at Jesus in the stained glass window, her unused handkerchief held firmly in both long-fingered hands.

I picked the daisies out of the sprays. One by one by one. Heart thumping, I sat down on the red carpeted steps and made a daisy chain, weaving the stems in and out, in and out, reminding me of the number 8 and how Mama said we were like that, winding around and through each other, not sure where one picked up and the other left off. Pastor Dave must have given up on his speech because he stopped talking again, and after a short silence,

3

the organist started "In the Garden," which I recognized from one of Mrs. Greene's Elvis records. Everyone stood, a commotion of creaking wood and turning pages, like they were glad for some direction.

I set the daisy crown right on top of the closed coffin lid, where Mama's head rested underneath, and then walked past Grandma, past all those other people who were studying their hymnals, singing for dear life. Right past Mrs. Greene, who reached out her hand so that I could brush mine against it, palm to palm.

The singing quieted as the door shut behind me. I sat down on the cold concrete steps under the eaves and watched the slush come down. "One Mississippi, two Mississippi, three Mississippi . . ." Drowning out the never-ending hymn.

Lacey followed and sat next to me, quiet. She took my hand in hers, our fingers intertwined like a chocolate-and-vanilla swirl. I leaned my head on her shoulder.

"Sisters forever," she said.

I couldn't make a sound, so I just nodded.

It took Grandma two hundred and fifty-six Mississippis to come outside. I didn't care it took her so long, though. Because I had a mama who never would have let me get past ten. We knew how to save each other.

2

Birds of
Sorrow

Mama said she started living the day I was born, and
when I was little, I took that as the literal truth. It was only
ever the two of us, so I figured the stork dropped us down as
a pair. The very first picture in our family photo album was
of her, sitting up straight in the white sheets of a hospital
bed, looking down at my little pink face and curly brown
hair like she couldn't quite figure out where I came from
but she was happy just the same. No childhood pictures of
her. None of her pregnant. Just her and me in that hospital
bed, dropped down together from some kind of heaven.

When I got to school, of course, I saw that most people had all manner of relatives. I didn't have to change
my theory much, though. I decided that me and Mama
were alone because the other pieces of our family broke off
somewhere on the way down, and if Mama kept moving
us around like she did, we'd run into them somewhere.

By that time I was seven and had been telling anyone
who asked about my theories on the stork and my lost

family. But it wasn't until second grade, when I gave Christopher Wales a black eye for telling me I was bonkers, that Mama finally cleared things up.

She was working on a junk-art bird at the kitchenette table in our tiny apartment, her long blond hair held back with a clip. Where I always managed to hang out my tongue or squinch my eyes when I was concentrating, Mama's face was still and pretty. She'd been building junk-art birds, mostly cranes, since before I was born. Making those birds was a cross between pure love and a nervous habit, the way some might do crossword puzzles or needlepoint. She sold them in the restaurants where she worked or at small flea markets and coffee shops for a little extra money. I thought they were the most beautiful creatures I'd ever seen and always felt a twinge when they flew away to their forever home, wishing we'd find ours.

She patted the metal folding chair next to her and smiled at me, a closed-lipped smile that hid a crooked tooth. As she went back to work inserting the rivets that closed the small metal body of the bird, she tried to explain a little about how babies come and that I'd had a daddy and grandparents once. I didn't want to believe her. My Stork Theory had been with me so long, it was almost like a friend.

But curiosity about the rest of my family won out.

"Where are they?" I said.

"Your daddy and grandpa died before you were born."

She stopped her riveting and swallowed a bunch of times, like their dying was caught in her throat. It stopped me, too, having to give up the idea of them so soon.

Mama toyed with the pile of spoons she always found a way to work into her birds. The late-afternoon sun shone its slanted light through the window, the winter dirt on the outside stealing some of its shine.

She went on to tell me they'd died together in a car accident, that my daddy had loved me every bit as much as she did. She walked to her dresser and brought out a small framed photo of her sitting in a patch of wild daisies next to a young man who had my high forehead and lopsided smile. His name was Scott. Then she picked up the slim volume of Robert Frost poetry she'd been reading to me every night since I was born. *A Boy's Will*, it was called.

"This is all I have left of him." He didn't have a family, she said. They'd died in a house fire when he was sixteen.

"What about Grandma?" I said, hopeful.

Mama sighed. She told me they had always fought like cats and dogs, and that her being young and pregnant was just too much for Grandma. She wasn't one to face things, Mama said, and so Grandma sent Mama on a bus to live with another family in Texas, "until they could figure out what to do next." Mama got off the bus in San Diego, California, and she'd been looking for the perfect home for us ever since.

It didn't occur to me right away that Grandma must be a horrible person, someone I wouldn't want to know. All I thought about was the idea that there was someone out there connected to me by blood. Someone we might belong to besides each other.

So I fired questions at Mama. Did you ever get along with Grandma? Where does she live? What did you and Grandma fight about? Do you think we'll ever see her? Why doesn't she come find us?

Mama took my face in her small hands and told me that thinking about where she came from was painful for her, even still. And I didn't want to be paining her, now, did I? "Because we take care of each other, right?" she said.

"But Grandma's still out there somewhere?"

"Yes."

"Doesn't she want to know where we are?" I swallowed hard. "Or who I am?"

Mama pulled me into her lap and her yellow chair creaked under our weight. "You have to trust me, Grace. We don't need anyone else."

So I believed her. Plus, I didn't want to add to her pains by bringing it up all the time. It seemed to me that

8

Grandma must have been a pretty terrible mother to send her own daughter packing while she was so young and pregnant. That made her mean. Small-minded. I decided right then and there she wasn't worth a speck of love.

Mama set me back on my chair. Then she went to the same dresser where she kept the picture of my father and took out a black-and-white-checked notebook. She set it on top of the Robert Frost book.

"Here," she said. "Sometimes it helps to write about things that make you sad."

I eyed her skeptically. "You're just trying to trick me into writing practice."

She laughed and the dark mood lifted.

"You caught me."

But I figured it couldn't hurt. So I wrote down some wobbly seven-year-old words.

Fly away sad feelings.

Each of her birds held a sorrow or a wish—all her sleepless nights and worries, all her hopes for the future—formed into words and sketches tucked deep inside those birds and meant to fly away. Before that day, I didn't know what she might be worried about, what might have made her feel sorrowful. I only understood my own sorrows, the way they would settle into the empty spaces meant to be filled by other things—a father, a place to call home—and I didn't know how to scrape them out.

Mama offered to let me tuck my words into the bird she was working on. But I wanted to keep them. They were mine. I wrote down more words that day, and most days since.

That was how I saved myself.

TRACY HOLCZER spent her first twelve years in San Jose, California, with her boisterous Italian family. *Everything Else in the Universe* is a love letter to that family, the pink kitchen where she discovered her nonni's secret ability to infuse food with love, and the San Francisco Bay Area in all its foggy glory. *The Secret Hum of a Daisy* is her critically acclaimed first novel. A full-time writer, Tracy lives in Los Angeles with her family, one fluffy dog, and four (yes, four!) cats.

You can find her online at
tracyholczer.com